Montana Mistress
SARA ORWIG

First published in Great Britain 2010
Large Print edition 2010
Harlequin Mills & Boon Limited,
Eton House, 18-24 Paradise Road,
Richmond, Surrey TW9 1SR

ISBN: 978 0 263 21576 2

Harlequin Mills & Boon policy is to use papers that
are natural, renewable and recyclable products and
made from wood grown in sustainable forests. The
logging and manufacturing process conform to the legal
environmental regulations of the country of origin.

Printed and bound in Great Britain
by CPI Antony Rowe, Chippenham, Wiltshire

SARA ORWIG

lives in Oklahoma. She has a patient husband who will take her on research trips anywhere from big cities to old forts. She is an avid collector of Western history books. With a master's degree in English, Sara has written historical romance, mainstream fiction and contemporary romance. Books are beloved treasures that take Sara to magical worlds, and loves both reading and writing them.

With love to Hannah, Ellen, Rachel, Colin, Elisabeth and Cameron.

Prologue

"**T**his is August, and next May the time is up for our bet," Chase Bennett said, gazing at his two favorite cousins as they relaxed at a table in the VIP lounge of the busy Chicago air terminal. "Hope you guys have been productive."

"Don't worry about us," Matt Rome replied easily with a twinkle in his blue eyes. "You take care of yourself."

"Our newlywed here probably can't think, much less get out and earn a dollar. He's in love," Chase teased, drawing out the last words as he raked his dark brown hair away from his forehead.

"I think he just married to get her money," Matt added, glancing at his watch.

"None of us would go to that length to win," Jared said. "I didn't expect to marry, and I know neither of you do. Life is full of surprises. Money wasn't why I married Megan, but it's a nice plus on the side. When we made our bet to see who could make the most money in a year, I had no intention of losing, marriage or no marriage."

Chase swallowed the last of his coffee. "I'm glad we were all in Chicago at the same time. You fellows are difficult to catch. If you'd get out of Wyoming more, cowboy, we could get together."

"I'll get out of Wyoming. Just let me know when and where," Matt said, finishing his drink and standing. "My plane is ready and waiting. We'll leave as soon as I'm on board, so I better go. Good to see you guys."

Jared stood, dropping bills on the table. "That's for the drinks. I'll see you guys at Christmas. In the meantime, keep working. Or give up. Either way, I'm going to win in May."

"You may be in for a slight surprise," Chase said, smiling.

"You think your new oil discovery is going to flow liquid gold into your coffers. You have to get it out of the ground first, and you're not absolutely certain it's as big as you think. In short, you don't have a sure thing," Jared said with a good-natured lightness.

"Dream on, cuz," Chase answered, unruffled because the three had competed since they were small boys. He held out his hand to shake with each cousin. "It's been great to see both of you. We're doing better about seeing each other this year, but having a wedding helped."

"Don't count on me for another one," Matt said. "I think both of you know better than that."

"No wedding in my future, either," Chase said. "Jared, you have our sympathy, you poor sap."

"Neither of you know what carnal delights of marriage you're missing," Jared said, and both Chase and Matt rolled their eyes.

"Go on back to the little woman," Chase instructed. "Matt and I will take our single life." They paused in the hallway. "I've got an appointment soon, so I have to run. I'm spending two more days here before I go on to Montana."

"See you, Chase. Take care," Matt said and waved as he walked away with Jared, who called goodbye again.

Chase headed toward the front and his waiting limo. In spite of the good-natured teasing, he intended to win the bet with his cousins. He thought he had the best chance of winning, but he knew it would be stiff competition. He thought about Jared's recent marriage, a surprise. No marriage loomed anywhere in his future. He was never falling into that trap.

One

"**B**e nice to the man." Laurel Tolson repeated the words of her red-haired hotel manager, Brice Neilsen. She gritted her teeth. "Be nice, be nice, be nice." She recited the litany to herself, glancing at her bare ring finger but seeing the 14-carat diamond that Edward Varnum had given her. She pictured Edward's flashing blue eyes, remembered being in his arms and then she clamped her jaw shut.

Today, the first week in August, another wealthy playboy, the oil magnate Chase Bennett, was coming to her hometown of Athens, Montana. She wanted no part of him, but over the next few weeks she was going to have to feed and entertain him and his executives, and she would have to be as friendly as Brice had cautioned.

Glancing at her watch, she planned to return to the hotel in less than two hours, since Chase Bennett should arrive later and she wanted to be present to greet him. She imagined he would travel in the same manner that her ex-fiancé had, in a limo with a staff at his beck and call.

As she drove along a wide street of Athens, she reflected on how she had grown up in a friendly place. The small town had none of the bustle and traffic of Dallas, her current residence. Tall black walnut trees and pines shaded the street, and wide lawns surrounded the two-story frame houses that always meant home to her.

She inhaled the crisp, fresh air and turned into the hospital parking lot, saying another prayer that this day her father would come out of the coma. Each time she thought about him, her insides clenched. How it hurt to see him lying immobile in the hospital, because her dad had always been strong and filled with vitality.

Taking another deep breath, she squared her shoulders. She loved her father—as did everyone who knew him. He was an elegant charmer, full of fun before his stroke last month.

When she turned into an empty parking place at the hospital, the roar of a motorcycle interrupted her thoughts. Glancing over her shoulder, she watched a deeply tanned man race past her, his dark brown hair ruffled by the wind. He wore a red bandana around his forehead, a tight T-shirt and jeans. She frowned slightly at the noise he created in a hospital lot, but then she forgot him as she climbed out of her car.

Inside the hospital she greeted front desk attendants and hurried through an empty corridor to enter an elevator. She pressed the button for the fifth floor, but before the doors closed, a booted foot stopped them.

The doors opened automatically, and she recognized the biker when he stepped into the elevator. She couldn't stop staring. He was strikingly handsome. Tall and broad-shouldered, he dominated the small space with a commanding air as if he were in charge of the entire hospital. The thought crossed her mind that few women could keep from noticing that his snug T-shirt revealed muscles and the tight jeans hugged narrow hips. Adding to his rugged appeal was his dark brown hair, a tangle from the wind with locks falling over the red bandana. His sunglasses were pushed up on his head. His thickly lashed, startling green eyes were his most breathtaking feature, and she could imagine how easily women succumbed to them.

As he turned to make eye contact with her, she was held immobile in his riveting gaze. Electricity crackled between them, and she wondered if he was aware of the aura that surrounded him. She suspected he was fully cognizant of his effect on women.

He smiled, revealing creases that bracketed his mouth and softened his features. It was an enticing, coaxing smile and had probably melted feminine hearts as easily as his bedroom eyes.

"Hi," he said in a deep voice.

"Good morning," she replied. She couldn't recall ever seeing him before, and no female could possibly forget him or avoid noticing him.

"Can you tell me where the Tolson Hotel is located?"

Startled by his question because she had come from the hotel, she nodded. "Yes, you're almost there now. Two more blocks to the west and one block to the east. You're not from here, but you're visiting someone?" she asked, wondering aloud why he was in the hospital.

"I have a friend who flew in last night and had emergency gallbladder surgery. I'm here for a visit. You can come with me and meet my friend if you want to verify my story," he said with a twinkle in his eyes, and she could feel heat flush her cheeks.

"Sorry. It's not often you find solitary strangers in this hospital, because people know each other throughout the area—whether they live on a ranch or in town." As soon as the elevator stopped at the second floor and the doors opened, the stranger didn't move. When she glanced at him, he merely smiled.

"You're going to miss your floor," she remarked.

"I've decided to ride up and back down again so I can talk to you. I didn't expect to meet a beautiful woman, and I have a few minutes. I don't see a ring on your finger."

"No. You're observant," she said, not caring to discuss herself with a stranger.

"After you finish your visit, it would be nice if you'd show me the downtown area because I've never been here before. I don't know anyone, and my friend won't be getting out and around. I'd like to take you to dinner afterwards."

She smiled back at him. "Two blocks beyond the hotel is the Athens Chamber of Commerce and the tourist bureau. If you'll go in there, you can arrange for a walking tour and they will answer your questions about our town."

"That is definitely not what I had in mind," he said, looking more amused. "If you're worried because we're strangers, I can give you some of my background and you can meet my friend. If you show me around, we won't be alone. We'll be on foot in public. Where's the danger in that? Unless you have a better place to suggest, I'll take you to dinner in the hotel later—still very public."

"Thank you, but I have commitments. Try the Tourist Bureau."

"So, when this elevator stops on the fifth floor, you're going to walk out of my life forever?"

"I'm afraid so," she said, smiling at him while she stepped closer to the door. "You'll get over it," she added lightly. He moved closer to her and she inhaled, catching the scent of an enticing aftershave.

"You're breaking my heart," he said in a lower tone. "And your name is?"

"I think we'll remain anonymous strangers. And I'm sure you won't have any difficulty finding someone to show you the town."

"What makes you think that?" he asked with great innocence.

She laughed. "We're a friendly place, and you're not bashful," she replied instead of answering truthfully that she was certain he could find several women who would be more than glad to escort him around Athens.

He smiled in return. "If you live here, I suspect I'll see you again."

She nodded. "Perhaps you will," she answered, half tempted to toss aside caution and show him the downtown. She gazed up into his eyes and knew she was making the right choice, but she had regrets. This stranger might be an antidote for Edward and their breakup.

The elevator stopped and she stepped out.

"Goodbye, until we meet again," he said.

She waved and went on her way, her thoughts on her father, and the stranger ceased to exist.

Feeling helpless and hurting, for the next hour she sat at her father's bedside, relieving the private-duty nurse the family had hired. As machines regularly pumped and an IV dripped, she watched the monitors steadily charting his condition, which wasn't changing.

"Dad," she whispered once, touching his hand. "I'm here. We want you to come home," she said, tears filling her eyes. "I'm selling the hotel and a potential buyer is arriving in town soon," she said quietly.

Knowing her dad couldn't hear her, she stopped talking. A charmer, her dad had a huge weakness that she had learned about in college, two years after her mother had died—he loved to gamble. But she hadn't known the full extent of it, that it was a compulsion and that he owed large sums of money.

She mulled over the shocks and changes that had occurred in the past month. First the devastating stroke, and then before he had lapsed into the coma, he had held her hand and, with tears in his eyes, confessed to her that he'd had huge gambling debts he had covered by mortgaging the hotel and getting a smaller loan from the bank with their family ranch as collateral. Sounding anguished and so unlike himself, he had told her that he didn't know what they would do if something happened to him.

Laurel had promised him she would take care

of the others and told him to not worry, that they would be all right. Then he'd lapsed into a coma and the future had changed.

Except for family, very few people in the area knew about their finances. Their banker, a lifelong friend, and his staff had been privy to the confidential information about her dad's loans. Yet no one but the bank president knew the loans were for paying off gambling debts.

The hotel had been mortgaged to the hilt, and if she sold the Tolson, she would use the money to pay off the mortgage. When she sold the Tall T Ranch, she could pay the smaller loan against the ranch and hopefully, have enough left to buy a home in Dallas for her family and help her sisters go to college. She intended to make as much profit as possible on both the hotel and the ranch.

Her father's secret about the gambling debts was safe with her, and she prayed that the bank would keep their business confidential.

Glancing at her watch, she picked up her purse and stood. "I'm going back to the hotel. I love you." She bent to brush his cheek with a kiss.

Wiping her eyes, she went out the door, talked briefly with the nurse and hurried to her car. She ran a couple of errands, then called the ranch to talk to her grandmother and younger sisters. Next she spoke to their ranch foreman and finally headed back to the Tolson Hotel, which had been built more than a hundred years earlier by her great-great-grandfather. The six-story honey-colored Montana limestone structure was ornate, clearly belonging to another era. As she walked through the lobby, she noticed with satisfaction the oriental rugs on a highly polished chestnut plank floor, potted palms and deep red leather furniture. Hurricane glass fixtures added to the turn-of-the-century ambience. In the hall to her office, she spotted the tall, blue-eyed Brice and motioned to him to join her in her office.

She put away her purse in the antique, hand-carved mahogany desk as the manager knocked and entered her office, crossing the room to take a chair facing her. Brice was nattily dressed in a charcoal suit for the arrival of the VIPs later in the day.

"I take it His Highness hasn't arrived," she said.

"I know you're stressed, Laurel, but remember, be nice to the man." Smoothing red hair that already was parted with every hair in place, Brice shook his head. "They say trouble comes in threes, and you've had your three, so maybe the arrival of Chase Bennett will turn out to be a blessing and solve some of your problems if he buys the hotel."

"I know," she said, sitting behind her desk and tapping her finger. "I expect another Edward and I didn't see any limos out front when I arrived."

"He may be another Edward. Don't hold that against him. Chase Bennett is worth a billion and he's intent on buying property here because of his new oil field, so smile at the man. He's a handsome bachelor and you're single and pretty."

"Thank you, Brice, but believe me, the last thing on this earth I'm interested in is another playboy." She shuddered.

Brice made a steeple of his hands. "You're sincere about that, aren't you?"

"Yes, I am. What's so difficult to understand?"

"Don't bite my head off. If you're so worried about the girls and your grandmother and your dad's health and medical bills, a rich friend or husband would solve your financial problems."

She shook her head. "Sorry if I snapped at you, but another Edward wouldn't be worth the money. I'll take my responsibilities as they come."

"How's your dad?"

"He's the same. Thanks for asking."

"Your dad is a strong man. I think he'll come through this."

"Thanks for the encouragement," she said, knowing Brice was always the optimist. "Do you think everything in the hotel is ready?"

"As we'll ever be. The hotel looks marvelous—and it's summer, so we have it almost totally booked through August, although that part may not interest him. I'm sure he'll have no problem filling rooms. A lot of his people are here because they've already started working on the new oil field." With a glance at his watch, Brice stood. "I'll be in the kitchen, making certain all our supplies have arrived."

"Thanks for all you're doing." She nodded and stood.

"You're welcome. It's my job. Please remember—"

"Be nice to the man," she finished for him. "I'll try my best. After all, I need to sell this place desperately. If I do, I want to tell Dad even if he won't know it."

"I understand," Brice replied, smiling and giving her a look filled with sympathy.

When they parted, she rode the elevator to the suite she occupied on the top floor. Chase Bennett had reserved the other two suites, which included the largest suite that ran along the entire south side, plus half of both the east and west sides of the hotel. She guessed he would take the larger suite of the two he'd booked and assumed his closest associate would take the other.

She stepped out of the elevator and was surprised to see the biker from the hospital emerge from the second elevator. Dark locks of his wind-blown hair still fell over the red bandana wrapped around his forehead, and his aviator shades hid his eyes. He had no luggage with him.

"I see you found the hotel," she said, wondering what he was doing and if he had followed her.

Removing his sunglasses, he turned to her. The moment their gazes met, the chemistry that had sparked earlier between them ignited again, even hotter this time.

"Yes, thanks," he answered easily, walking toward her to stop only yards away.

"I'm sorry, but this floor is occupied," she said. "These are suites and they're all booked."

One corner of his mouth lifted in a grin. "The desk clerk said I'd be on the sixth floor."

She smiled. "What's your room number? You're probably on the fifth floor," she said, realizing he might work for Chase Bennett.

He fished in a pocket. "Believe it or not, I have a suite on six."

"I believe you," she said, reassessing him and guessing he was in Bennett's company. Red flags of warning went up in her mind. This handsome, sexy stranger was too appealing. He was probably almost as wealthy as his boss and someone she should guard against getting to know well, even though she suspected few women wanted to shield their hearts or anything else from him.

"Do you work for Chase Bennett?" she asked.

"Indeed, I do. I think it's time we introduce ourselves," he said, holding out his hand, his green eyes dancing with wicked mischief. She wondered if she had offended him earlier by turning down his invitation to show him the downtown—a legitimate request if he was one of Bennett's employees.

"I'm Chase Bennett," he said as she extended her hand and his closed around it.

Two

Shocked, she stared at him while his warm hand enveloped hers, sending tingles spiraling through her.

"Oh, my! You don't look like your pictures. I think I made a dreadful mistake this morning," she blurted, feeling her cheeks flush.

"You can make up for it," he replied in a deeper voice that filled his words with innuendo and stirred another sizzle.

"And how can I do that?" She couldn't resist flirting in return, speaking in a sultry tone that made one of his dark eyebrows arch. Desire was obvious in his expression.

"Have dinner with me tonight," he said.

"I'd be delighted and I'll show you our town," she replied, aware of her hand still held in his while his thumb ran lightly back and forth across her knuckles. Her emotions churned because he was another moneyed womanizer, and distaste curled in her with a sour urge to keep as much distance as possible between them. On the other hand, she wanted to win him over in hopes he would like the hotel and buy it.

"Deal," he said. "And your name is—?"

Her cheeks flamed again as she realized she'd forgotten to introduce herself. "I'm sorry. I'm doing everything wrong with you."

"Not at all," he drawled. "You shouldn't be expected to recognize me from my pictures," he added, combing his hair back from his face with his fingers. Now she could see the resemblance, but she realized she never gave a thought to the possibility of a biker being Chase Bennett.

"I'm Laurel Tolson," she said.

"Of the hotel?" he asked, waving his hand to take in his surroundings.

"Yes. You reserved two of the suites on this floor."

"I thought I had the entire floor," he remarked with surprise in his tone.

She shook her head. "There are three suites, one large and two smaller, and I live in one of the suites. If you really need this entire floor—"

"Ah, that's even better," he interrupted. "You and I will have this floor to ourselves," he said, his voice once again becoming deeper.

"You have both suites for yourself?" she asked in surprise.

"Yes. I like privacy. Look, I have to clean up. Are you free in about half an hour to show me around the hotel?"

"Certainly. I'll be happy to do so," she answered briskly, withdrawing her hand from his. "We can eat in the hotel's main restaurant, and it'll be complements of the house."

"I believe I asked you to dinner, not the other way around," he said, looking amused again.

"Maybe we'll do that another time. Let me show off my hotel tonight," she coaxed, smiling at him as he flashed a smile in return that made her knees weak.

"That's also a deal," he said. He glanced at his watch. "Let's make it three o'clock. Which door is yours?"

"Give me your keys and I'll show you your suites," she said, holding out her hand.

As he placed two small plastic cards in her hand, his fingers brushed hers, a light touch that she noticed. She crossed the hall, aware of him beside her and then holding the door for her to enter after she unlocked it. "Does this look satisfactory?" she asked, turning to him.

"Beyond my wildest hope," he replied, his gaze on her. She realized he was again flirting.

Trying to hang on to her patience, she smiled. "I'm referring to the suite."

"Ah, the suite," he said as if he had forgotten anything else existed except the two of them. When he looked around, she did also. She noted with satisfaction the chilled bottle of champagne in an ice bucket along with the large platter of hors d'oeuvres she'd ordered to be sent to his suite the moment he checked into the hotel.

Two baskets of fresh flowers from the local florist lent a festive air, and she decided everything was the best she and the hotel staff could possibly achieve. He glanced around at the marble and mahogany tables, the red velvet upholstered chairs and camelback couch, the paintings in gilt frames and the hurricane lamps, the fireplace and its granite mantel. His gaze returned to her.

"Very attractive," he said politely.

"Thank you. Even though this is an old hotel, we try to stay first-class and have attempted to maintain the historical ambiance. I can imagine the luxurious places you've stayed."

"This is excellent. I know there are meeting rooms downstairs. Is there a desk anywhere in my suite?" he asked, prowling the room like a cat in a new home.

"Yes. It's in the bedroom," she replied, leading the way. "If you want it moved, we can do that easily." She stopped in the center of the bedroom and motioned toward an antique rosewood desk, which was less ornately carved than the one in her office. She was suddenly very aware of the high-backed cherry wood king-size bed.

Looking around, Chase stood with his hands on his hips, and he dominated the large bedroom as much as he had the small space of the elevator.

"The desk is fine in here," he said.

"Good. If you'll come with me, I'll show you the other suite."

He stepped close and held out his hand. "You don't need to bother. Give me the key. Is there an adjoining door?"

"No, there aren't any adjoining doors between the suites. You'd better let me show you which of the other two suites is yours, so you don't try to get into mine."

"And that would be bad?" he asked.

"I'm not worried, Mr. Bennett," she answered with a smile.

He stepped closer and ran his finger along her shoulder. She could detect his aftershave again, and her nerves tingled from his proximity, but it was his finger touching her shoulder that stirred desire.

"No 'Mr. Bennett,' please. It's Chase," he said in a warm tone. "You and I are going to get to know each other and not on a professional basis," he said. "We'll start today, even though the first hour will be business."

"We'd be much better off to keep things impersonal and on a business basis," she stated briskly, wondering if she was saying that for her own benefit.

"I can't think of one good reason why we'd be better off on an impersonal basis for our friendship." He caught a lock of her hair that had come loose from its clip. He toyed with the blond strands, winding them around his finger.

"I hope it's up close and personal and business has nothing to do with what happens between us as a man and a woman. A beautiful woman whom the man wants to know."

She laughed. "I find that a real stretch, but I'm looking forward to dinner tonight."

He touched the corner of her mouth, tickling her slightly. "Ah, I'll have to make you laugh often. You have a great smile."

"Thank you," she said, heading for the door.

"Show me which suite is yours, so I don't try to get into the wrong place."

She stepped into the hall, getting out her own key. "Right there," she said, pointing. "How's your friend in the hospital?"

"He's doing fine, and if he were home, he'd be released today, but since he's here, I've made arrangements for him to stay in the hospital another two days at least. Once he's released, he'll fly home in my company plane with someone accompanying him."

"That's good. I'm glad he's recovering."

"May I see where you live?" Chase asked.

"Of course," she said, thankful she had picked up her things earlier. She opened the door to her suite and they entered a smaller living area with blue-upholstered mahogany furniture instead of red.

He turned to look at her. "You realize I'll know where you live and what it's like."

"They're all similar with a few variations in decor."

He walked up to her again, stopping close. "I'm looking forward to this afternoon and tonight. When you stepped off the elevator at the hospital, I thought it might take me days to find you."

She smiled at him. "You were going to search for me? I'm flattered."

"Yes, I was. A fabulous-looking woman. A chemistry between us—which I know you feel," he said in a raspy voice. "A woman who was a challenge to me. How could I resist trying to find you?"

"I'm not a challenge, Chase," she said, aware of saying merely his first name. Already they were on a personal, first-name basis and had scheduled an evening together. She knew she wasn't exercising the caution she had intended to use when she met him. It could easily be Edward all over again except Chase Bennett did not seem the type to get engaged.

"You turned down my invitation in the hospital," he reminded her.

"And you're not accustomed to getting turned down or to hearing 'no,' are you?"

He shrugged. "I hear it, but if it concerns something I want, I go after it anyway. Unless it's a woman who doesn't want me around. I won't intrude. But if there's a fiery chemistry that both of us feel, I'm not going to back off that one," he said and ran his fingers lightly across her hand.

"Well, I haven't said no this time. I don't go out with strangers, so that was why I refused earlier. You come with all sorts of credentials. We've got an afternoon and evening together, so I'll get ready."

One corner of his mouth lifted in a crooked smile. "I can take a broad hint like that. I'm leaving and I'll be back at your door at three."

He closed the door behind him and Laurel let out her breath. She had done everything wrong with him, but he hadn't seemed bothered that she had turned him down at the hospital or had assumed he couldn't be the occupant of one of the suites.

She went to find something to wear and to

shower again. Even though her pulse raced when she was around him, she didn't want to spend the evening with him; she had to keep reminding herself of the purpose behind all this—it was an opportunity to promote the hotel. So far she had to admit that in most ways he wasn't another Edward. She expected to find that arrogant, "I-own-the-world" attitude manifest itself soon enough. And there were similarities: Chase was brash, filled with all possible self-confidence, as determined to get his way as Edward had been. Chase happened to like motorcycles and Edward liked limos. Each could afford whatever he wanted, and she guessed they felt the same where women were concerned.

Also, she suspected the limos would appear before long. And she was certain he was far more of a womanizer than Edward, who had none of the sexy charm of Chase Bennett. She'd read about Chase in tabloids, in the Dallas paper and in magazines, and he'd always had a beautiful woman at his side—but she'd never noticed the same one twice.

Searching through her closet, she selected a simple burgundy linen dress that was sleeveless and ended above her knees. She laid out high-heeled sandals. After taking down her hair, she shook her head to let it fall freely across her shoulders and then pinned it high on each side while her thoughts were on Chase Bennett and his fabulous smile. He was getting ready to spend the evening with her. What were his plans for the night?

Chase let the warm water pour over him, closing his eyes and raising his face into the spray. In minutes he turned his back to the gushing water. His thoughts were on Laurel Tolson. He had been surprised when he'd learned who she was. His staff had researched the town, the properties for sale and the hotel, but no mention had been made to him of the owner except that Radley Tolson had had a stroke and was in the hospital and his daughter was handling the hotel in the meantime.

She was a stunning willowy blonde with luscious curves, and she had flirted briefly with him this afternoon, although it was after she'd discovered his identity and not before. This always sent warnings that the woman might be far more interested in his fortune than in him. She wanted to sell him her hotel, and from what his staff had told him, the hotel had a large mortgage, while the Tolson ranch was three-fourths paid off. She wasn't without funds, but whatever she had would be paltry compared with his worth.

He had first noticed her as she was walking into the hospital and he'd hurried across the parking lot to catch up. He'd been intrigued by her blond hair, which looked fantastic in the sunlight. That and her enticing walk and long legs. Maybe he'd spent too much time without a woman, but he'd been caught up in work 24/7 for more than the past month.

He had rushed to avoid losing sight of her, barely stopping the elevator doors from closing, and then had met her gaze and been riveted. They had a chemistry between them that he hoped to explore.

She had been cool and unreceptive, yet in spite of her aloof manner, she had sounded breathless.

He grinned, remembering how she'd seen him as a biker and discounted that he could be Chase Bennett. To her own embarrassment. She said she had done everything wrong with him, but it had merely amused him and he had not been offended. When she had flirted, his interest had escalated.

He wanted her in his bed. Soon. As he shaved,

he continued to think about Laurel. She was single, which surprised him. Friendly toward him, once she knew who he was. She wanted to sell the family hotel to him—that would give him some leverage—and he suspected that was why she'd accepted his dinner invitation. He could still picture her standing in the elevator, trying to remain cool and aloof but exuding an air of awareness of the chemistry between them. While still wearing his sunglasses, he had looked her over carefully, starting with her silky blond hair clipped behind her head, her thickly lashed blue eyes and her creamy skin. Her plain white blouse had clung to full curves and then was tucked into a narrow waistband of a tan skirt ending above enticing knees. He could envision her long, shapely legs wrapped around him. From that first moment he had been interested in her. Then he'd removed his shades, looked into her eyes and received an electric jolt that held the heat of a lightning bolt.

Just thinking about it aroused him. He wanted her naked, pressed against him, beneath him in his bed. Why hadn't she married? he wondered, yet he didn't care. He just knew that while he was here, he intended to seduce her.

It had been awhile since the last woman in his life. And he'd been happy to tell Carole goodbye. He recalled the tall blonde he'd had the last affair with. She'd been sexy, cooperative, enticing at first. But then she'd become too clingy, and he'd been happy to break it off permanently. Work had easily replaced her, and he'd all but forgotten her. Maybe that's why Laurel was having such a strong effect on him—because he'd gone too long between women.

Beautiful, sexy women were easy to find, but when it began to get serious, he wanted out. No getting locked into a life of routine for him. Seven or eight months with one woman and he began to get edgy and want his freedom. Often much sooner.

Chase raised his face to the water and then shook his head. Tonight he would be with Laurel. Anticipation heightened. He turned off the water, stepped out and wrapped a towel around his waist. Picking up his cell phone, he called Luke Perkins, his Senior Vice President of Land Administration, to come upstairs so they could talk.

Chase walked into the closet, which had already been filled by his staff. He chose a navy suit and tie and a white shirt. As he dressed, he realized that Athens was small and since everyone would know everyone else, he'd be able to find out Laurel's history easily if she didn't tell him tonight.

At a knock on the door, Chase called out "Come in," and Luke Perkins strolled into the room. His tall, black-haired vice president had been with Chase from the earliest days, and Chase could always count on Luke's judgement.

"Have you looked over the hotel?" Chase asked as he stepped into loafers, combed his straight brown hair and put on his watch, glancing at the time to see he still had twenty minutes before he was to meet Laurel.

"Yes. This hotel is overpriced for its age. Of course, it's probably priced that way as a point to start bargaining from, and I'm sure she doesn't expect to get her asking price. Her father, Radley Tolson, is in the hospital in a coma, but she has power of attorney and has been appointed his guardian, so she can do what she wants and it's all legal. The grandmother and Laurel Tolson's two sisters live on their ranch. This family settled this area in the territorial days in the nineteenth century. The family ranch is for sale also."

"Know why she's selling their property?" Chase asked.

"The real estate broker and the banker both think she's selling because of her father's health," Luke replied, stretching out in a wing chair. "He oversaw running the ranch and the hotel. Now even if he survives this stroke, his health is gone. She's made a life for herself in Dallas. There's the grandmother and younger sisters to care for. From what I've heard, it's a close family and this daughter is in charge now."

"A real family person," Chase said with coldness. He tried to avoid getting involved with anyone into commitment or family, which amounted to the same thing. They wanted to extend that commitment to him. He valued his bachelor freedom, and he wasn't getting into the marriage trap his parents had been in, tied down constantly. He'd watched them grow older without ever getting to do anything except farm and raise their family.

"That's right. She's a landscape architect with her own business in Dallas. She was engaged to Edward Varnum."

Chase stopped combing his hair and turned to look at Luke. "Edward Varnum? I know who he is, but I've never really been around him. He inherited a fortune that his grandfather made and his father increased. His grandfather patented some kind of equipment that goes in every plane ever made. That was the start. Now he has multiple international enterprises. They're no longer engaged?"

"No. I think it's a fairly recent break, but from what I understand, Edward is definitely out of her life."

"So, she's on the rebound. Know whether she did the breaking up or Varnum?"

"No. I haven't heard any rumors yet. I'm sure I will."

"I'm meeting her at three and she'll show the hotel to me," Chase remarked, and Luke headed toward the door.

"I better clear out. We have an appointment with her in the morning, and she's taking five of us on a tour. I'm surprised she didn't wait and lump you in with us tomorrow, but maybe this is a personal, individual tour where she can try the hard sell."

"Have you met her?"

"Oh, yes," Luke replied, grinning, his gray eyes twinkling. "She's a real head turner. Don't forget, this is a business deal."

"I'll remember. Did you leave the folder with all the figures in it for me to read?"

"I did," Luke answered, motioning toward the desk.

"Are we still set to drive to the field Wednesday morning?" Chase asked, putting his billfold into his pocket and picking up keys.

"Yes, we are. I'll see you later, Chase." As Luke closed the door behind him, Chase crossed to the desk to retrieve the folder and read the figures for the hotel. Gazing out the window, he thought about the new oil discovery and the land and mineral rights he'd acquired. His fortune was going to grow. Here in this quiet, sparsely populated state, oil would flow and money would be made. His thoughts jumped to the bet he had with his two closest cousins: whoever could make the most money by next May would be the winner, with each man putting five million dollars into the pot. With this oil field he hoped to win. Forgetting about the bet, Chase envisioned Laurel's blue eyes and her smile. He closed the folder and left his suite, crossing the wide hall to knock on her door.

When the door swung back, his pulse accelerated. She'd let down her blond hair in the back in a silky fall. The simple lines of her dress were perfect to emphasize her beauty.

"You're gorgeous," he said in a husky voice.

"Thank you," she answered, smiling at him. "Come in and let me switch off my computer."

He stepped inside and watched the sway of her hips as she hurried away from him.

The burgundy dress was straight and hugged her hips. He imagined her without it, noticing the long zipper down the back of the dress and wishing he could take her into his arms right now to pull down that zipper.

She smiled at him as she approached. "Is this strictly business tonight, or part business, part pleasure?"

"Definitely pleasure with you," he said.

"If you'd like, we can go downstairs to the bar and have a drink first, complements of the house. This will be an informal evening as far as business is concerned."

"Forget work other than showing me around," he said, the purchase of her hotel the last thing on his mind. He could worry about that later and let his efficient, reliable staff get the pertinent facts.

As he held the door for her, he inhaled a whiff of an exotic perfume and noticed the slight swing of her shimmering blond hair. Taking a deep breath, he fell into step beside her.

"Tell me about the hotel," he said when they were in the elevator.

"My great-great-grandfather built the original hotel in 1890. Billings was founded earlier than Athens, and the railroad went through there. Later a line was laid from Billings to Athens, and we're also on the river," she said, gazing up at him with wide blue eyes that captured his concentration. "Then the hotel burned and this one was constructed on the same spot in 1902," she continued. "Two years ago my dad had it remodeled and refurbished. So with that, you have our history."

"The hotel's history. Not Laurel Tolson's. I intend to learn that, too."

"It's not nearly as colorful and nothing out of the ordinary. I grew up in Montana."

"We have that in common. So did I."

"Did you really?" she asked, sounding surprised. "I thought you were a Texan."

"I live in Houston now, but our family home is a ranch near Dillon. That's where I grew up."

"It's a pretty part of the state. So we do have things in common. I grew up here in town and also on a ranch. That same great-great-grandfather is the one who acquired the land we have. He managed to keep the hotel and ranch going, and the generations since have been able to do the same."

"Do you live in the hotel all the time or on the ranch?"

"Actually, like you, I live in Texas. I have a landscape business in Dallas, and I did the land-scaping for the hotel."

"Later, we can take a walk outside and I'll see what you've done."

When they emerged from the elevator, she led the way to a darkened bar with large mirrors, low lighting, walnut paneling and dark walnut booths and tables. A small dance floor was at the opposite end of the room from the ornately carved bar. So far, all he had seen of the hotel had exceeded his expectations. He hadn't anticipated anything terrific in the small ranching town.

Sitting at a corner booth, Chase faced her and thought about the coming month. When they'd discovered the rich oil field where he held leases and mineral rights and owned the land, he'd thought good fortune had fallen in his lap. After meeting Laurel, he considered himself doubly fortunate. From that first moment he had been captivated by her.

A small light glowing on the table threw a warm, rosy glow on her and was reflected in her crystal-blue eyes. His gaze traveled down to her mouth, and he wondered what it would be like to kiss her. He vowed he would know before the night was over.

"I saw a dance floor as we entered the bar. What time does the music start?" he asked.

"After eight every evening. We have a small band that plays, so it's live music and mostly old favorites with some rock and western thrown in."

"Then we'll come back later tonight and dance. In the meantime, tell me more about the hotel and the town," he said, leaning back and opening his navy jacket.

Their waiter arrived, interrupting the conversation. "Chase, I want you to meet Trey, who's been with us for a long time," Laurel said, and Chase greeted the waiter. "Anytime you're in the bar," she continued, "he will see that you and your staff are well taken care of, so let him know what you want." She turned to her employee. "Trey, this is Mr. Bennett, who'll be our guest."

"Welcome to the Sundown Bar," Trey said. "Here is a wine and drink list." He placed a thick black folder in front of each of them. "I'll give you a moment to look it over."

Chase nodded, and she looked at hers although he suspected she knew it from memory. She shoved aside the menu at the same time Chase closed his. "Now, back to your interest in the hotel and the town," she said.

"Where do your guests come from? People driving through town, people on vacation? Is there anything that draws people to this town specifically?" he asked, looking at the V-neck of her dress and wanting to slide his fingers beneath it and caress her.

"The hunting and fishing and dude ranches draw tourists. We have a rodeo that attracts people."

"I'm interested in a comfortable place for my employees to stay and in seeing to it that they can get good food while they're here," he said. The hotel was comfortable and held a degree of charm, harking back to another era, but he was far more attracted to the owner than the hotel.

"I think you'll find this a well-run and well-staffed hotel. We have excellent dining, which you'll taste tonight and can make your own decision," she said. "My dad always made a special effort to get and keep superb chefs."

"Good sales pitch," Chase said, leaning forward. "Now tell me about yourself."

"I already have," she replied, and he shook his head. "There's not much to tell. My dad's in the hospital, and my grandmother and two younger sisters live on the family ranch."

"Do you mind my asking why you're selling?"

She glanced away and he reached across the table to take her hand, feeling another jump in his heartbeat the instant he touched her. "I can tell that question caused you pain, so ignore it because the only thing I need to know is that the hotel is for sale."

When she smiled again, he realized he could get addicted to her smiles, which warmed him each time.

"No, if you're considering buying it, you have a right to ask because for all you know, there could be rumors floating around that it's haunted."

"Are there rumors?"

She shook her head. "Not at all. I'm selling for my dad's benefit. He's in a coma in the hospital, and even if he recovers, he won't be able to manage the ranch and the hotel the way he had in the past. My grandmother cares for my two younger sisters, but my grandmother is getting older."

"So you're a family person," Chase observed coolly, remembering his conversation earlier with Luke. Laurel Tolson was the kind of woman he usually avoided getting entangled with. She was the type for marriage. He always thought of all the years he'd watched his parents locked into responsibilities and cares that had turned them old ahead of their time. That kind of commitment wasn't for him and gave him chills. "You're making sacrifices in your own business to take care of your relatives."

"Yes, as a matter of fact, I'm very much a family person," she said with a bite to her words. Anger flashed in her blue eyes. "I've taken responsibility for my family in my dad's place. I intend to take care of them financially as well as otherwise."

The last was stated with a chip-on-her-shoulder attitude, and he wondered about the breakup of her engagement. Had Ed Varnum offered to take over the finances and she had refused to let him, creating a wedge between them? She seemed highly independent, and he could imagine her turning down less than acceptable offers. He tucked away the question, determined he would get the answer.

"That's commendable," Chase said, looking at her full mouth and knowing he wasn't going to back off getting to know her better. He always made it clear he wasn't into commitment, but this was one woman he wanted to make love to in spite of her apparent opposing views on relationships.

"What I'll do depends on Dad's recovery, but eventually, I hope to either get my grandmother and sisters settled in town here or move them to Dallas. My business is good and growing, and I don't want to leave it. I can have a much better business in a big city like Dallas than here."

"True enough," Chase remarked and then paused as Trey returned for drink orders.

When they were alone again, Chase leaned forward to take her hand once more, compelled to touch her if he possibly could. He glanced at her bare ring finger. "How long ago did your engagement end?"

"It's been a month now."

She looked surprised. "I see you've done some research on me."

Recent," he said. "I hope you're not sour on all men."

"Hardly," she replied, smiling at him.

"Good news. There's no other man in your life?"

"Heavens, no! Actually, I've been too busy for anything else. I try to spend some time each day at the hospital with my dad. We've hired a private-duty nurse to stay with him, but all of us go to see him often, even though he doesn't know it."

"Sorry to hear about him," Chase said.

She held his gaze for a moment and nodded. "I've been overseeing the hotel, and I get out to the ranch for the weekends. I live here during the week. Right now, with you in town, I'll be here at the hotel."

"Selfishly, I'm glad, but I'm sorry to take you away from your family," he said, brushing her hand lightly with his fingers. "I had no idea I'd find Montana so fascinating."

"Let me introduce you around. If you'd like, I can have a reception here at the hotel so you can meet the locals."

"That would be good because we plan to be here off and on for most of the coming year and while I don't wish your father ill, I hope you don't go back to Dallas soon."

"There's no danger of that."

"Who keeps shop there while you're away?" he asked, looking again at her lips and wondering about kissing her. He wanted their dinner to be over so they could dance and he could hold her in his arms.

Trey returned with a bottle of chilled Chenin Blanc to uncork, and she withdrew her hand from Chase's. After tasting the wine, Chase gave his approval; he waited until the wine was poured and they were alone again to raise his drink.

"Here's to Montana's spectacular ladies, particularly the one I'm with right now."

"I find that difficult to drink to—a toast to myself," she said with amusement. "Here's to Montana's economy growing through your efforts," she said, lifting her glass. "That's what I'll toast."

"If you sell the hotel, since it's been in your family so long, won't that be a heart-wrenching sacrifice for you?"

"I can't look back or cling to the past. I doubt if you do either and I'm sure your life has changed a great deal, hasn't it?"

"Sure. I don't recall anything that was a big sacrifice in mine. I was happy to get off the ranch and into the world of finance," he answered, admiring her for what she was doing to take care of her family. Because, in spite of her answer, selling the hotel had to hurt.

"You must enjoy the career path you've chosen, too," he said. "I guess when you were engaged, you'd planned to give it up when you married."

"Actually, no. I don't have to be present constantly to keep it running—that's what I'm doing right now. I'm sure you can juggle yours when you're away."

"That's right. I just figured you would want to let it go."

"Not at all. Everyone here is excited about your Montana discovery. You'll see how happy when you meet people."

"With you to introduce me, I'm sure they'll be friendly." He paused. "So where did you go to college?"

"K-State for a degree in landscape architecture. I wanted to go farther south, but still some place I could get to and get home, something that must not have mattered to you," she replied.

"Nope, and I had a great scholarship offer from Texas A&M."

"So was Edward your first love?"

"Actually, no. There were boys in high school,

but I wasn't really serious with them, and one in college, but we never got engaged. I don't even need to ask you because I can guess—and you have far too many pictures that showcase your life."

As they chatted, he noticed she continually shifted the conversation to either an impersonal topic or a focus on him, trying to steer away from talking about herself; yet little by little he gleaned tidbits about her.

When they finished their drinks, she said she would show him around the hotel. He walked beside her, inhaling her perfume and wishing he could link her arm in his or better yet, put his arm across her shoulders, but he didn't want to rush things, because she had a definite barrier in place.

They circled the attractive grounds in front, which had thriving plants that were well suited to the northern climate, and he was impressed with her landscaping. The patio with a heated pool was equally inviting, and he could imagine how appealing it would be year-round if it had a retractable roof.

Finally they went to the dining room and were seated for dinner, where Chase met more of the wait staff.

"I suppose you know what you want for dinner," he said.

"I have favorites, but I'll look at the menu again," Laurel replied.

"Tell me what you recommend," he said as she skimmed over the listings of entrées.

"The steaks are delicious. I particularly like the rib-eye. I like the roasted pheasant, and I think our fish is tasty. The cedar plank salmon is a favorite of most regular diners."

They lapsed into silence for a few minutes while they read menus. Chase closed his to see that she had already put hers aside. "So you grew up on a ranch, too," he said, eager for more personal information.

"Part of the time. Otherwise, we lived at the hotel so we could go to school here."

Their waiter returned and as she gave her order, Chase was able to look her over slowly, mentally peeling away the burgundy dress, his imagination running riot with erotic images. He was impatient to hold and kiss her, yet he was enjoying getting to know her. So far, his first impressions had been accurate, and he was still intrigued by her and wanted her more than ever. He tried to stop thinking about how long it would be before they could dance and he could take her into his arms.

After she ordered the Madeira-roasted pheasant with mango sauce, he was aware of her watching him when he ordered the rib eye.

The minute they were alone, he took her hand in his; she glanced down at their hands. "This isn't a big city or even a large town. Everyone knows everyone else, and you'll start wild rumors by sitting here and holding my hand or if we dance tonight."

"First, is that bad? Do you mind?"

Smiling, she shook her head. "Not really because it means nothing to me. It will be forgotten fast enough, and I don't mind the questions."

"Maybe it means a little more than 'nothing,'" he remarked, and her eyebrows arched as she shook her head.

"It can't possibly. We don't know each other, and there isn't anything between us," she said with emphasis, and his suspicions strengthened that she was sour on relationships. Only a month ago she had been planning a wedding, so her attitude was no surprise. And no real hindrance as far as he was concerned. If she was sour on relationships, that would make life easier for him, because she wouldn't be focused on wringing a commitment from him. This was actually good news.

"I thought there were women, or at least *a* woman, in your life," she continued.

"Currently, not at all. You said no men in yours, either, and I take it your fiancé is definitely out of the picture?"

She nodded. "Positively, and he won't be back in it."

"So, we're both free and can enjoy getting to know each other. I know I am now," he added softly, wondering what she was thinking and what her expectations were for the evening.

She smiled at him, yet he felt a coolness and that she was merely being polite. The waiter returned with a basket of freshly baked rolls, their iced teas and tossed salads, and she withdrew her hand from his with another smile at him. He wished it promised something more later, but he knew better. Their entrées arrived, and his juicy steak looked cooked to perfection the way he had ordered, and her pheasant appeared equally enticing. After the first bite, he took a sip of his iced tea. "My compliments to the chef."

"We budget extra to get one of the best chefs in this area—as far as I'm concerned, he is the best chef. He's from St. Paul and had enough of city life. Dad has been delighted with him, and if you'll notice, the dining room is filled and there is a line of those waiting. People come from the surrounding area to eat here—the customers tonight aren't hotel patrons exclusively."

"Good recommendation for your hotel."

"The pièce de résistance is the Chocolate Sin dessert, which I've already ordered," she said. "You'll see when it arrives."

"An enticing dessert named 'Sin' in your hotel? Intriguing. What other sinful things will I find here?" he asked, dropping his voice and leaning closer over the table.

"I can tell that you're hoping the owner is, but alas, no one would describe me in that manner."

"It doesn't mean I won't, does it?" he asked. She inhaled and something flickered in the depths of her eyes.

"Chase, darlin', maybe I should change my lifestyle and add a little excitement to it," she drawled, slanting him a look and licking her lower lip.

"Laurel," he whispered, suddenly burning in the cool dining room. He knew she was flirting and had replied to him in fun, but as he drew a deep breath, he had to fight the urge to take her hand, get out of the busy dining room and go where they could have privacy.

She winked at him. "Calm down, Chase, I'm teasing," she said in a brisk voice, but that didn't wipe out the past moment and her flirting. He couldn't wait to get through dinner—his appetite for food had fled.

Twenty minutes later their waiter appeared and set a dessert in front of each of them. Chase gazed at the mountain of dark chocolate, ice cream, chocolate syrup, brownie, sprinkles of walnuts and whipped cream with a red cherry on the top. "Absolutely luscious," he said, looking directly at her and not considering the dessert when he made his remark. "And before the night is over, I'll see how sinful," he added in a deep voice.

Again, something flickered in the depths of her eyes, and he suspected her pulse was racing as fast as his.

"What's sinful," he said softly, "is what we do to each other. Only I intend to do more and I hope you do, too."

"Eat your dessert, Chase. That's all that is wicked here," she instructed, picking up her fork.

She ate little of hers and he ate only half of his even though it was fabulous. He was more interested in dancing with her now that the band had begun playing.

Finally, they stood, and this time he linked her arm in his to return to the bar. "Now we'll dance."

"I believe I promised to show you our town after dinner," she said.

"I'll take a rain check on the tour of Athens. I'm interested, but I want to dance with you now."

"Whatever you'd like," she answered without hesitation. "Your real estate agent has probably already taken you around more than once."

"Actually, no. Anyway, that would be entirely different from you showing me," he said, smiling at her as they entered the darkened bar.

They sat in the same booth they had occupied earlier, because she had told Trey they would return and to reserve it for them. As they waited for her iced tea and his cold beer, Chase glanced around the packed room. "This has to be more than hotel guests."

"It is."

"Good music, nice place—you have a great hotel. I'm impressed."

"Why do I think you're being polite?" she asked. "I suspect it takes much more than our century-old hotel to really impress you," she said.

"Not when the owner is a stunning blonde," he replied and took her hand as he slid out of the booth. "Let's dance, Laurel."

Three

With mixed feelings of caution and a bubbling excitement, Laurel walked to the dance floor with Chase for an old ballad. As they threaded their way through the crowd, she gazed at him. Handsome with enticing eyes that would melt ice, he was too hot-blooded, too charming, and she could feel the barriers around her heart crumbling. And she was certain he was aimed at seduction.

Why wouldn't he? He knew the effect he had on women. He liked women and he was charming and wealthy, a combination that made him totally irresistible.

Yet she intended to withstand his appeal and keep up her guard because she was certain that there was nothing long-term in his intentions. She would be a temporary fling to entertain him while the new oil field was being developed.

And he was absolutely another Edward, one more jet-setter who wanted life on his terms and thought only of himself. Never again would she be so gullible.

Chase definitely desired her and was coming on strong, but then he had leverage because he had something that she wanted—she hoped he would buy the hotel.

She wouldn't let herself think about the possibilities, but he could afford her asking price and he was going to buy property here anyway, although there were other places and he could afford to get what he wanted.

Every time she thought about him making an offer, she focused on a different subject because she didn't want to have to deal with the enormous disappointment if he didn't make an offer.

Even so, it was difficult to keep from speculating and hoping. Equally impossible to withstand his charm.

He was magnetic and sensual, and something inexplicable stirred a fire between them. She'd never had that before with any man and couldn't understand it. Nor did she want it. Not with this man, of all people. Why couldn't it be Frank Durbin or Kirk Malloy or one of the other locals who was reliable and so much like her that any of them could have been a brother? But maybe that was part of why there were no fireworks with any of them.

On the dance floor Chase drew her close into his arms. His aftershave was enticing. He was warm and his crisp cotton shirt smelled fresh, but it was their touching each other that took her attention. She was aware that their slightest contact stirred physical needs.

Sex had never been great with Edward. He had wanted her and pursued her, pouring attention on her and showering her with gifts, dazzling her until she had been blinded and thought they had something solid together.

How wrong she had been! She didn't intend to fall into the same trap twice, although she couldn't imagine Chase ever marrying or pursuing her in the manner Edward had. Yet she knew Chase had seduction on his mind and wanted her in his bed. He had made that obvious, and while her intentions to resist seduction, as well as falling in love, kept up emotional barriers, her body responded and she succumbed to the fun of flirting with him.

As they danced, she became acutely aware of their legs brushing and their bodies lightly pressed together.

Then the number ended and a fast one started. She watched his enticing moves. He loosened his tie, his heated gaze traveling slowly over her, and she tingled from head to toe.

Circling him, she wondered whether she could maintain his interest in purchasing the hotel yet stay out of his bed. She intended to try to sustain that balance and keep her body to herself. As she watched him dance, she reminded herself that she was flirting with disaster. Chase's narrow hips gyrated to the heavy beat, and she imagined him in bed and realized she was going to be incredibly tempted. With every move the man was sexy. He flirted, he charmed and his green eyes beguiled. How was she going to hold him at arm's length while flirting and dancing and soon…kissing him?

The thought of kissing him made her heart race. Looking at his full, sensual lower lip, she wondered what it would be like. The room warmed and she became breathless, more so when she glanced up to meet his knowing gaze.

One lock of dark brown hair had fallen over his forehead, reminding her of that slightly wild look that he'd had when she'd first seen him.

At the end of the dance, he took her hand to go to their booth. "I have to shed this jacket," he said, pulling it off and hanging it on the side of the booth before turning to take her hand and head back to the dance floor for a slow number.

By midnight, she was wrapped in his arms, dancing close against him, and he had talked her into going out with him tomorrow evening.

"What time does the bar close?" he asked.

"Not until two in the morning. Two more hours," she answered. "But we won't be here that long because I have to get up early."

"This is enjoyable, but let's call it a night as far as the dancing is concerned and go up for a nightcap." He leaned back. "How does that sound?"

"Fine with me," she replied. If only he were an ordinary Montana cowboy, she would be excited and happier to be with him. As it was, she was on edge, wondering if they would each be working to get what the other wanted.

As they left the bar, he draped his arm across her shoulders. In the elevator he watched her with a smoldering gaze. Certain that kisses were inevitable, she wanted him to kiss her. Otherwise, she was afraid he would vanish out of her life and her hotel. His kisses should be reasonably harmless and a good antidote for Edward, she thought, knowing she intended to kiss Chase tonight.

When he looked at her mouth, she couldn't catch her breath. The elevator stopped and still watching her, he took her hand and they stepped off.

"Want to come to my place for a nightcap?" she asked and he nodded. He took her key card and opened the door.

Only one small lamp burned in her suite. Chase placed the key on an entryway table and turned to look at her. His eyes filled with fiery, blatant lust as he reached for her and drew her to him.

Her heart thudded when she walked into his embrace, winding her arms around his neck and raising her mouth to his as his head came down and his lips, his tongue, met hers. Setting her ablaze, he kissed her while she pressed against him and wound her fingers in his hair. His sizzling kiss, deep and thorough and demanding, was so much more than she'd expected or ever known before.

With a desperate urgency, she clung to him and met his fervor. As he held her, desire increased enough to destroy reason and control.

Chase swept her up into his arms and carried her to a couch to hold her on his lap. His arousal pressed against her hip, and her body arched in response. She wanted him.

His hands moved to her zipper, and then he pushed her dress off her shoulders. With the rush of cool air on her bare skin came lucidity.

"Chase, wait—we're going way too fast," she gasped, glancing up to find his gaze on her breasts, which were covered in a lacy pink bra. Pulling her clothing back in place and gathering her wits and caution at the same time, she tugged up her dress.

"Zip me, please," she whispered. "We've just met. This is too soon for me."

Nuzzling her throat, he trailed kisses to her ear. His warm breath and lips dissolved her protests. Holding him, she relished his mouth grazing her throat, until she realized how easily she had succumbed again.

She grasped his upper arms to push him. "Chase—" she whispered. "Just wait a little. Let's catch our breath."

He raised his head to look into her eyes and she trembled. His desire was unmistakable, blazing in the depths of his eyes. "You're fabulous, Laurel," he replied, his words melting her.

He ran his index finger across her lips, adding to her longing.

"Chase," she said, "let's get something to drink and cool down."

He gazed at her intently, and she wondered if he'd even heard her. He wanted her and it showed as much as if he'd announced it.

"Laurel, come here," he said and slipped his hand behind her head to pull her closer as his mouth came down on hers for another kiss.

Her toes curled and her arms wound around his neck, and in spite of the brief pause she kissed him as passionately as before. Time spun away while he held her close against him.

She had no idea how long they kissed, but she knew when he ran his hand over her hip and along her thigh, and then beneath her skirt. She took his hand and pushed against his chest, breaking away and wriggling off his lap.

"You go so fast that you take my breath."

"Your kisses are what take my breath," he declared. He stood and placed his hands on her waist. To keep him at a distance, she put her hands against his chest, but that wasn't what she really wanted to do. She longed to wind her arms around his neck, stand on tiptoe and kiss him again.

She put her finger over his lips to quiet him. "Stop saying things like that, because you know that's as seductive as your kisses. Let's get something to drink and put some distance between us."

"Why?" he asked, nuzzling her neck.

She moved away and took his hand. "Come with me," she said, gazing into his eyes. Her heart drummed and she wanted him more than she should.

With a solemn expression, he followed her. Still on fire from his kisses, she dropped his hand as she led the way into the small kitchen, where she switched on lights and motioned to him to sit.

"I'll help," he said, getting glasses while she got a pitcher of tea she'd made earlier. He filled glasses with ice and she poured tea, all the time aware of him moving around her, brushing against her lightly, keeping her breathless. "Lemon or sugar?" she asked.

"Neither," he said, shaking his head. "I don't

even want tea," he added, and she glanced at him. "I want you, Laurel." He set both glasses on the table and turned to take her into his arms, and she couldn't protest any more than she could walk away from him.

"Let's start the evening early tomorrow. How about four? You can show me the town and then we'll eat afterwards," he said. "This time I'll take you somewhere."

"Chase—"

"A few extra hours—that's all. Let's get to know each other."

She wanted to kiss him, and dinner tomorrow night was a distant appointment that she barely gave thought to. "Yes," she whispered, slipping her hand across his nape. She craved his kisses, something she had intended to avoid. Instead, she was hopelessly lost with wanting him.

Standing on tiptoe, she kissed him ardently and once more was swept away by heart-pounding kisses she wanted to continue all night.

Finally, she paused. "Chase," she gasped, trying to get her breath. "You either go or we sit and drink our tea. We can take our drinks into the other room."

While they stared at each other, she wondered

what he debated. "Is this a problem? Are you that unaccustomed to hearing a woman say no?"

A smile briefly flitted across his features. "Actually, maybe I am. I was wondering if I ought to walk out and leave you alone from now on, but that isn't what I want to do. I like a woman in my life, but I want her to choose to be there."

"I'm happy to get to know you, but we were moving into a more intimate relationship too fast for me."

"Get to know each other, it is," he said. He picked up his iced tea and walked back into the living area.

Sitting and talking, they sipped tea until two in the morning, when Chase stood. "I better let you get some sleep."

Keeping distance between them, she followed him to the door. "I'm scheduled to meet with your staff at ten o'clock. I'll show them the hotel. Will you join us?"

"If you're there, of course," he said. He reached out and slipped his arm around her waist and drew her to him. "This has been a fabulous evening, but it's your kisses that are sensational. You know you've killed all chance of sleep, unless—"

"Don't even say it," she whispered. "You go and you will sleep."

"Have breakfast with me," he said.

She hesitated a moment and then nodded, thinking breakfast wouldn't be filled with temptation and she could talk some more about the merits of the hotel.

"The whole evening was fantastic," he said.

"I agree, Chase," she replied softly, and they locked gazes again, yearning building with each heart-pounding second and then his head lowered and his mouth met hers.

She held him tightly, yet at the same time she remembered that this was the road to disaster. Finally, she stepped back. "Enough for tonight," she whispered. "See you tomorrow, Chase."

"How's seven for breakfast?" he asked.

"Fine."

He smiled and touched her cheek with his fingers before releasing her and leaving.

As she shut the door behind him, she took a deep breath, crossing the suite to turn off the lamp and carry empty glasses to the kitchen.

"He's Edward all over again. Don't for one second forget that," she lectured herself aloud, her words sounding hollow in the empty suite, trying to convince herself to use her good sense where Chase Bennett was concerned, yet her mouth tingled and her body clamored for him and his loving. "There's only a few degrees of difference in the two moneyed executives, Chase and Edward," she argued aloud, knowing her lectures were useless. Chase set her on fire with longing and need.

When she was ready for bed, she turned off the lights and pulled on a cotton robe, picked up a throw and stepped onto the balcony, where she curled up on a chaise and looked at town lights and rooftops while trees were dark shadows in the night.

Chase was far too appealing. She would have to maintain a balancing act—resist him yet keep him interested. Chase was by far her most likely prospect to buy the hotel, so she couldn't drive him away. Tomorrow she and Brice were showing Chase and some of his executives the hotel. Later her real estate agent would take Chase's staff again, to look at the hotel and answer any questions.

Sell him the hotel and combat his attraction. The latter was going to be the most difficult, she knew.

She stretched back in the chaise and closed her eyes, thinking about Chase's tempting kisses and mulling over the evening until she realized she would never get to sleep if she didn't get him out of her thoughts.

Impatiently, she tossed aside the throw and went to bed, running over chores involving the hotel until she finally fell asleep, only to dream about Chase.

Determined to be professional the next morning, she dressed in a tailored, seersucker, pale blue and white pinstripe suit and white blouse, looping and pinning up her hair. She wanted to appear serious, hoping to look like the owner of the hotel and a businesswoman and keep that image in front of Chase so he thought of her more that way than the woman he'd flirted with, danced with and kissed last night.

Promptly at seven, she heard a knock at the door and hurried to meet him.

Dressed in a gray knit shirt and slacks and western snakeskin boots, Chase stepped inside her suite, closing the door behind him. His brief scrutiny made her acutely conscious of her appearance, and her pulse speeded.

"You look luscious this morning," he said in a husky voice. He placed his hands on her shoulders.

"Thank you. You look quite handsome. I'm trying to be a businesswoman, and you know how you can help," she said, attempting to sound brisk, yet her voice came out breathlessly.

He grinned. "I don't have a clue."

"Oh, yes, you do," she said, tapping his chest with her forefinger, losing her struggle to sound all-business, because his aftershave was as enticing as it was the night before. Fresh and filled with energy, he looked as appealing as ever.

His disarming smile added to her defeat. "I've been looking forward to breakfast and being with you again."

"Thank you—that's nice," she answered politely.

"Most of all, I've been looking forward to one good morning kiss to make the world right," he said, sliding his arm around her waist and causing her heart to skip a beat.

"Chase, you can't—"

"Oh, yes, I can," he whispered and placed his mouth on hers; her protests died.

He kissed her fiercely and she forgot the

morning schedule or even why he was there. She wound her arms around his waist and held him close as she kissed him back. Her heart thudded while she forgot every resolution she had made in the night and early morning hours.

"Chase," she finally whispered, twisting away from him and stepping out of his embrace. "We have to stop."

"I don't know why," he said, caressing her nape and moving closer again.

Shaking her head, she placed her hand against his chest, feeling his racing heartbeat and realizing it probably matched her own. "Let's go to breakfast, act sane and remember a business meeting is the aim of the morning."

"That comes later," he reminded her with a cavalier manner that dismissed all her protests. "This is a private breakfast together, only us, and I can't resist you."

She wanted to say that was mutual, but she had no intention of confessing her reaction to him, although he obviously knew it. "We need to stay on schedule," she persisted.

"We are," he replied and kissed her again, and this time their kisses lasted longer before she finally stopped him.

"Now we have to go," she said, stepping away from him quickly.

He held the door and she walked out ahead of him. "Thank you," she said. "I think you'll enjoy our breakfast buffet, and as usual we attract diners who are not guests of the hotel, but you'll see why."

"Everything I've seen here so far is impressive," he said, and she smiled at him.

Returning to the main dining room, which was filled with morning sunlight, she moved ahead of him in the breakfast line that held glasses of various fruit juices, freshly cut melons, bright red strawberries and slices of green kiwi, yet all the tempting food couldn't take her attention from the man with her. Along with omelets, biscuits, sausage and strawberries, they chose steaming cups of coffee and chilled orange juice.

Leaving the line, they strolled outside on the patio, deserted in the early morning. As she set her tray on the table, she remembered the last time she'd had breakfast with a man on the patio—it had been Edward. And she was with another Edward this morning.

"Nice out here," Chase remarked, holding her chair and caressing her nape with his fingers, fueling the fire he'd kindled with his kisses.

"When few people are around, I love the patio," she said. "Early morning is the best time because the rest of the day and the evening, the place becomes busy and crowded."

"We agree on that. I like solitude."

"Are you an only child?" she asked, thinking she could look into his bedroom eyes all day.

"Hardly. I have five siblings, three brothers and two sisters."

"So there were six of you, and you're the oldest," she said.

"How'd you ever guess?" he asked with a grin and they both chuckled.

"Do you return home to Montana often?" she asked.

"Not during the past few years. I have a brother, Graham, who stayed on the ranch and a sister, Maggie, who lives in Montana, so they have family. There are four grandchildren, so far." Chase's prominent cheekbones left his cheeks in slight shadows. Wayward locks of his dark brown hair fell over his forehead, with the faint breeze ruffling them. He looked as if he belonged on the Harley more than in a boardroom, but she knew that first impression she'd had of him had influenced her. She might as well be seated across from Edward, she reminded herself, feeling that familiar curl of distaste; and in spite of Chase's torrid kisses, she hoped to maintain distance between them.

"My family is still on the ranch. My mom would like to sell and move to Florida, or let me take it over so they could live in Florida, but my father can't exist without work. When I was growing up, we took few vacations, except to get together with family. Mom has sisters and I have cousins. We could afford to take trips but didn't because my dad couldn't imagine letting a day go by without working. Nor would he turn his jobs over to another person."

"I'm afraid that doesn't run in my family," she said, smiling. "My dad loves a good time. He's a people person and everyone in the next six counties, plus here, knows him. That makes his stroke so difficult to accept," she said.

"Sorry. That's tough," Chase said, touching her hand lightly and sounding sincere, but she suspected that was part of his ability to convince people to do what he wanted. "You said last night you expect to be here in Montana for a while?" he asked.

"Yes. While I'm away, business will move

along without me because I have a competent manager in Dallas and a great staff. Right now my family needs me and I want to be closer to them."

"When you sell the hotel, will you move to the ranch?"

She shook her head. "Actually, if I sell, I hope I can make arrangements with the new buyer to let me stay here as long as I need to, so I can be close to the hospital and my dad. If not, I'll rent a place in town. I don't want to drive back and forth from the ranch to the hospital, and I try to go see him often. If Dad rallies, that will change because they will move him to a physical therapy center in Billings. We had already started making plans for the move but stopped because he lapsed into a coma."

"Sorry. You have the ranch for sale, too."

"We can't run the ranch without Dad, and I don't want the responsibility for it, therefore it's for sale. My grandmother and sisters live there now."

"And if it sells, will you move them here or to Dallas?" he asked.

"Well, it depends on my dad. I told him I'd like to move them to Dallas, but I don't know if any of them will want to go. Ashley is seventeen and can drive now, and Diana is fifteen. They may want to stay here. So may my grandmother. We'll have to see what we can work out for care for Dad." She smiled at him. "Now you know my family history and situation."

"And I've told you mine. So, what do you like to do? Swim, hunt, travel, movies—what?" he asked, reaching across the table to take her hand and run his thumb across her knuckles. She should withdraw it, but her reluctance crumbled in his presence, as usual.

"I swim. No hunting or fishing. Because of starting my own business, all my time is taken by my job."

"Not all," he contradicted. "You were engaged," he said. "Not that I care to delve into your past relationship, except to say that frankly I'm glad it's over. But that's a selfish view."

She thought that in addition to selfish, it was typical, knowing Edward would have been the same way had he been interested in her.

Chase's appetite seemed as poor as hers as they ate only a few bites, and she tried to avoid thinking about their morning kisses.

"If I'd known you were running this hotel, I would have come to Montana more often than I have and stayed here," he said.

She smiled at him. "I find that difficult to believe. I know there have been women in your life recently because I've seen a picture somewhere. Maybe more than one picture if I remember correctly."

"Whoever she was, she's been out of my life quite a while."

"You always end the relationship, don't you?"

"Obviously, or I wouldn't still be single. I'm not a marrying man. I don't want to be tied down like that."

"In other words, you've never met a woman you couldn't live without," she said, thinking he was coldhearted. "You sound scared of commitment."

"Terrified by it," he replied easily. "I'll admit it. I don't want to be in the trap my parents were in. Not ever. No relationship is worth being tied down all your life the way they have been. So am I alarming you?"

She smiled. "No. I have no intention of losing my heart to you. You've given plenty of warnings about the dangers of loving you."

"Maybe I've overdone it," he said, with a sparkle in his eyes. "I'll have to make up for that. I'll bet I can show you a good time if you'll give me a chance."

"I think I'm already doing that," she answered lightly, knowing they were moving away from his admission of fear of commitment. And now she understood a little more about him and his past. It actually was a valid warning to avoid emotional entanglements with him. Her brain was clearly on target. If only her heart was.

Soon he had her laughing over stories about starting in business, and she shared some of her experiences until she glanced at her watch.

"Chase! We're going to be late. It's time to meet the others."

With a smile he came around the table to hold her chair, and she noticed that he was undisturbed about the time and didn't hurry. She realized that everyone would wait for Chase's arrival regardless of when he showed up.

In the main lobby his staff already had gathered, along with Brice.

"Laurel, this is Luke Perkins, Senior Vice President of Land Administration," Chase said upon joining the group. As she shook hands with Luke, she noticed a wedding band on his finger and was grateful for the married men in Chase's party who would be able to keep focused on business. "And this is Dal Wade, Vice President of Marketing for our northern division," Chase added, and she shook hands with a stocky, blond man who also had a friendly smile. She greeted Brice, who stood between the two vice presidents.

Next, she met a vice president of Purchasing, an executive accountant and a Billings real estate broker, Sam Kilean. She introduced Chase to Lane Grigsby, her real estate agent, who had already met all the others.

Finally, when all the introductions were over, she led them to one of the smaller meeting rooms, where they had coffee and a continental breakfast, which neither she nor Chase touched. Aware of Chase's steady attention, she took turns with Brice telling the group about the hotel and answering questions.

She glanced at her watch. "We'll break for ten minutes and then meet again in the main lobby. Brice and I will give you a guided tour of the hotel. Any more questions?"

There were none and as the men stood to leave, Chase strolled around the table to her. "Appealing presentation. Maybe I should try to hire you."

"Thank you. If you have an interest in hiring a landscape specialist, we might have a discussion, but for anything else, I'd be out of my field," she said, smiling and realizing they were alone in the meeting room as she gathered up folders and papers, placing them in a neat stack to retrieve later.

He ran his fingers across her nape. "We'll get into the landscape possibilities later. That would be in Houston, not here."

"I have a capable staff."

His gaze bore into her. "I promise you, if I hire you, it won't be your competent staff I want."

She smiled. "I'll remember that and I'm sure you'll make it clear."

He grinned and ran his hand along her high collar, tracing it down to the vee of her tailored blouse until she captured his hand. "You've figured out that much about me, so far," he said.

"I've discovered a lot about you," she snapped, for a moment letting her animosity show and thinking about his wealthy persona that would want to have his way constantly.

One dark eyebrow arched and his eyes filled with a curiosity that made her cheeks heat. "I touched a nerve," he said. "We hardly know each other. You're not getting me mixed up with Edward, are you?" he asked with a shrewd perception that disturbed her.

"In many ways, I'm certain you're really quite different," she said coolly. "Your ten-minute break is vanishing, and I think I should run to the ladies' room before the next segment of our schedule."

"Of course," he said, and she hurried away, feeling her back prickle and suspecting he was watching her and speculating about what had rankled a few minutes earlier. She didn't have to stop in the rest room, but she had wanted to end the conversation between them that had taken a bad turn.

Starting at four, she would be alone with him again. She would be spending most of the day and evening with him. This was going to be an incredibly long week, perhaps a month or more, and already she was edgy from dealing with Chase.

Emerging from the ladies' room, she hurried to the lobby, where Brice was talking with several of Chase's men. As she strolled toward them, Chase turned to watch her, and beneath his gaze she tingled from her head to her toes.

"I see everyone is here," she said after taking a swift count. "Gentlemen, we might as well get started with our tour of the hotel, and we'll begin with the kitchen."

It took an hour to complete the tour, and the entire time she was aware of Chase's undivided attention. As they viewed the kitchen, he had questions and she answered them, aware he was also paying attention to business. Finally, they gathered for a lunch in a private room, where he sat beside her. Afterward they had a break and then met in a conference room, where she and Brice answered questions until they broke up at two o'clock.

As everyone left and Lane promised to call her, Chase strolled to her side. "Thanks for so much information. That was a good presentation."

Inordinately pleased, she thanked him, aware of Brice moving around nearby. "Brice and I will be happy to answer any further questions. Your people have some appointments with various hotel staff that should give you more information."

He nodded and touched her wrist. "I'll come to your suite at four," he said quietly.

"Fine," she replied, smiling at him. As soon as the door closed behind him, she sat in a chair and kicked off her shoes. "What did you think?" she asked Brice.

"I think Chase Bennett is interested in you."

She gave Brice an exasperated look. "Let's stick to business. Did we influence them?"

"They seemed impressed by our presentation and the hotel, but I can't tell whether they're interested in buying or not. I suspect that they don't know and are waiting to hear from their leader to decide what he wants to do. After all, it will be Chase Bennett's decision, not theirs."

"True enough. Brice, I don't even want to think ahead about selling to them beyond what we have to do to present the hotel. It's like counting your chickens before they hatch. The money from the sale would be a miracle for me and help in more ways than anyone knows," she said, tapping her finger on the arm of her chair and thinking about her dad. "I'm scared to count on it until I have the signed contract in my hand."

"For your sake, I pray we get the sale," Brice said.

"If we do, do you think he'll let all our people go?"

"Who knows what he'll do, but it's difficult to imagine he won't come in here with his own crew."

"It would be easier to keep who's here. Do you think he'll tear down the hotel?" she asked, mulling it over in her mind and knowing Brice had no more clue than she about what Chase would do.

"I don't know him and I have no idea. He's friendly and easy to talk to and best-buddy type, but it's only skin-deep. He's got all his plans locked away in that head of his. I hope for your sake he buys."

"Even if it means you work for him? That's what I hate. That and a few other things."

Brice smiled. "Word gets around in a town like this, and I've had four offers from various places, the closest being the new motel out on the highway and another was from the new hotel in Billings. I'll get along and you know the kitchen staff will survive the transition. Someone is trying to hire one of them away from us constantly."

"I know," she agreed with a sigh. "I'm going out with Chase tonight."

"Why do I feel there's no enthusiasm in that statement, while more than half the single women in the United States would turn green with envy and jump at the chance?"

She smiled. "You're right. If I expect to get the sale, I can't tick him off and I have to be nice, but it's already a struggle. In fairness, sometimes it's not. He's a charmer, but that's what makes it difficult. I don't want another heartbreak."

"You won't have one. I've watched you grow up, and your dad always said you have a head on your shoulders. Get a nap and go enjoy yourself and give him another sales pitch tonight."

"Thanks, Brice, and thanks for all your help today," she said.

After he left, she sat quietly for a few minutes, staring at the door and thinking how fortunate she was to have Brice, who had worked for her dad for twenty-four years, starting when she had been three years old. Level-headed and thoroughly familiar with the hotel business, Brice kept the place running smoothly without any seeming effort, but that was the result of years of experience and handling problems before they got out of hand. With a sigh, she stood to gather her things and go to her suite to stretch out and sleep for ten minutes and then shower and dress for the evening.

She selected a black dress with a dramatic draped neckline and a straight skirt that ended above her knees. Stepping into high-heeled black sandals, she wondered where he planned to take her. She left her hair down, parting it in the center and combing it so it fell in a cascade across her shoulders.

When he arrived at four, she gave him a quick perusal. He wore a gray sport coat, charcoal slacks and a white open-necked shirt and was as stunningly handsome as ever. With each passing hour she knew him, his good looks made a bigger impact on her.

The moment he entered her suite, his gaze drifted down over her, and his eyes revealed his approval. "You look gorgeous," he said.

"Thank you," she answered politely, conscious of how much his compliment pleased her, even though she was certain it was probably said without thought.

"Laurel, let's go to my suite and have a drink. I'd like to talk a little before we go."

"Fine," she said, instantly curious. Her heart skipped and she wondered if he had an offer for the hotel. She banked all speculation immediately, terrified about getting her hopes high.

He held the door, closed it and looped her arm in his to walk beside her. His aftershave was enticing and his touch light but enough to make her tingle. In his suite she set her purse on a table and walked across the spacious living area, noting that new bouquets of flowers had replaced the others. She also noticed that he had a bottle of champagne on ice.

"Champagne?" she asked, surprised.

"Yes. I thought we'd celebrate," he said, shedding his coat and folding it carefully to lay it over the back of a chair.

"What are we celebrating? Our new friendship?" she asked with amusement, her curiosity increasing by the minute.

"Of course, along with your successful hotel presentation and your sales approach."

"Thank you," she answered. Inordinately pleased, she smiled, even though common sense told her that her casual presentation, occasional sales pitches and tours couldn't possibly have sold him on the idea of buying the hotel. He peeled away the wrapper around the bottle and popped the cork, picking up a flute to pour bubbling champagne and hand it to her.

When she accepted her drink, her fingers grazed his. "Thank you again," she said. "Both for the champagne and for your compliments about the sales presentations."

He poured himself a glass of the pale liquid, and she looked at the delicate flute in his well-shaped, tanned hands. "Let's talk about the hotel and what you expect and what I hope to get."

"I think you know all the particulars and what I want," she said. "We've been over that, with you, with your staff and with your real estate agent," she added, her heart starting to race with the realization that he was actually talking about buying the hotel. Maybe she was going to make the sale!

"Yes, you have," he said as walked to stand by the mantel. Turning, he raised his flute of champagne. "Here's hoping we can work out a fabulous deal for both of us."

"I'll drink to that," she exclaimed, moving close to touch her glass against his as their gazes locked and the tension wound tighter. Her heart raced and excitement simmered in her. While he watched her, his eyes darkened with desire. Her mouth went dry and her breathing became erratic.

Dimly, she was aware that he set his drink on the mantel and took hers from her hand to put it beside his. Then he turned to her, placing his hand on her waist. Sensibly, she wanted to protest, yet the words wouldn't come. Instead, she looked into his eyes and felt consumed by them as he drew her closer. When he leaned down to place his mouth on hers, her heart slammed against her ribs.

She slid her arms around his neck and clung to him. His kiss carried more than the knee-melting jolt of earlier ones. There was all the fire of a streak of lightning. What was worse, his sensuous kisses fanned flames more than ever. Never before had she experienced kisses like Chase's, and she didn't want him to be special or unique, yet her fleeting thoughts were easy to ignore. She wanted his kisses.

Finally, wisdom and caution nagged and she pushed against him, causing him to raise his head. Both of them were breathing hard, and for seconds they stared at each other.

"I want to make you an offer," he said.

Her heart missed beats while excitement shook her. Trying to gather her wits and at the same time thinking he was taking unfair advantage by kissing her senseless before launching into business, she inhaled and struggled to regain her composure. Stepping out of his embrace, she picked up her champagne flute to take a sip and give herself another moment before she listened to him. "Go ahead," she said, the moment becoming etched in her memory.

"You want to sell your hotel," he stated.

"Yes, you know that. That's what this is all about."

"Partially," he replied. "That's what you want. Are you able to make a decision about selling, or are your grandmother and your dad or even your sisters part owners?"

"It's my sole decision," she said and couldn't see any change in his expression. "Two years ago my grandmother deeded her part of the ranch and hotel to Dad. After his stroke, the first opportunity he was able Dad insisted I be appointed his guardian and be given complete authority over everything."

"Shrewd moves by both of them," Chase said. "Do you need to confer with your grandmother out of courtesy?"

"Not really. I'll tell her, of course, when I have an offer, but the decision is all mine. Do you want to buy the hotel?" she asked, unable to stand the suspense of waiting.

He watched her intently and for the first time, she wondered what he had on his mind. "I want to make you an offer."

Curious, she became concerned with the roundabout way he was leading up to what he planned. She wondered if he was going to quote her some ridiculously low figure. Or something else entirely, or to work for him and keep her hotel? "All right, Chase," she answered in a subdued voice. "What or how much do you intend to offer?"

"Half a million more than your full asking price," he answered.

Stunned and perplexed, she stared at him. All her senses sharpened, and she realized he had been building to this moment. Barriers rose, caution enveloped her and she perceived a threat to her well-being. At the same time, her curiosity mounted.

"I don't understand. You'll pay a fortune—so what is it you want?" she asked.

He took her champagne glass from her hand, setting it on the mantel beside his and holding her hand in his. "I want you. I've told you I'm not into commitment or permanent relationships, and I don't think you're into temporary relationships or a relationship without a commitment."

"I'm not," she answered flatly, going cold.

"I want to make you an offer we both may be able to live with. I'll buy your hotel, Laurel, for your full asking price plus half a million, if you'll agree to be my mistress for a month."

Four

She stared at him while her heart slammed against her ribs. Her fury ignited and swept over her with the heat of a raging fire.

Starting to answer, she yanked her hand away from him. Before she could state, "No," he placed his finger on her mouth, stirring a sensual awareness of him.

"Wait, before you refuse," he urged. "You think about it. No strings, no ties. My mistress for a month and then it's over. You'll get the price you asked for and then some, which you're not going to get from anyone else. Don't answer me now. Let's have our evening together, and you think about your answer and sleep on it. I'm not into marriage, now or ever, and at this point in your life, I suspect you aren't either. This arrangement would be perfect. You'll get what you want and I'll get what I want."

"Perfect for you perhaps," she snapped, anger brimming. "I can give you an answer, Chase—"

"Don't," he commanded quietly. "Keep your options open and think about it and your future and your family. I'm offering more money than you will get anywhere else, and it will solve some of your problems."

"There's a name for that. In short, sell my body to you." She flung the words at him with bitterness.

"If you want to put it that way, but not really," he answered in a tone that held a note of steel, and for an instant his friendly facade slipped, revealing the strong-willed man that he really was.

"A month is fleeting and temporary," he said. "I can court you and perhaps seduce you and have my month without buying your hotel or paying anything extra."

She tilted her head to study him. "Why don't you? It would save you half a million and maybe get you what you want, where this way isn't likely to."

"I don't want to wait, and you've already given me refusals—the day we met, remember?" he asked, one corner of his mouth lifting. Her fury increased, but this time it was at her own physical reactions to him, which she couldn't control.

"You don't want to invest any of your valuable time in a relationship, do you?" she countered, and he arched one dark eyebrow as his index finger traced the curve of her ear.

"You can put it that way, but it's more that I don't want to wait to make love to you," he answered in a husky voice. "I'm not that interested in your hotel, but it'll serve my purposes because I need something for my employees as fast as I can get it."

"They can rent the entire Tolson Hotel immediately, so that part of your argument isn't valid. You want what pleases you without waiting," she said with contempt. The wealthy, arrogant playboy had surfaced, as she'd expected. He sought instant gratification and was accustomed to getting what he wanted regardless of the means.

"Perhaps so. The whole idea isn't so preposterous—and think of the rewards. You aren't giving them consideration. Imagine having the hotel sold. I can pay cash for it. You're not really thinking about that aspect of my offer."

"I find it difficult to contemplate selling the hotel when it's my body you want."

He smiled and put his hands on her shoulders. "You concentrate on the prospect of selling your hotel and drop the other temporarily. That may change some of your thinking here."

"No, it—" His head tilted and he bent slightly as his mouth covered hers and stopped her argument while he kissed her again. His arm banded her waist, pulling her close to him. She started to push away and protest because she didn't want to kiss him, but as his tongue stroked hers, her arguments vanished. Sensations rocked her and she put her arms around his neck. In spite of being furious with him, she kissed him in return. She wished his kisses weren't fantastic, mesmerizing, erotic.

As she kissed him passionately, she suspected she was already spinning off into a world of heartbreak, but at the moment she didn't care.

The thought dimly crossed her mind that seduction was inevitable.

While he kissed her, he leaned over her and her arms around his neck tightened. Time and problems vanished. With his arm banding her waist tightly, his other hand caressed her throat, roaming down over her breast, rubbing her taut peak. Even through the fabric of her dress, she burned from his caresses, moaning softly and losing caution. Desiring him, she wanted barriers between them removed. She ran her hand down his back, then lower along his hip, conscious of his arousal.

Abruptly, he raised his head. "You want this, too," he reminded her. "Say yes, Laurel," he urged.

Her mind spun as she attempted to focus and think and ignore the clamoring of desire. Either way, he would seduce her. She knew that without any doubt, because beneath the onslaught of his hot kisses, her caution always faded.

With a shiver that ran from her lips to her toes, she stepped back and pulled herself together.

"You know you make me want you, but it's lust. Absolute lust."

"You think about our future and your hotel," he repeated softly. "C'mon. We'll go to dinner and get to know each other a little better."

Feeling as if she had lost round one in a fight, she silently picked up her purse and left with him. Waiting at the curb was a sleek black limo and she thought of Edward. Only Chase was not Edward. Chase was sexier, more charming and a shark. He went after what he wanted with less subtlety than Edward but with even more determination. And even more assurance he would get it.

Her thoughts churned over her dilemma and her decision. He had presented his offer and then shown her why she might as well accept it.

Half a million above her asking price! The amount dazzled her, and she tried to avoid consideration of what she could do with the money for her family. Half a million versus becoming his mistress. Weighed against the temptation of his offer, her distaste and anger simmered over his arrogance.

She studied his handsome profile, which kept her pulse racing. No matter how hard she tried or how annoyed he made her, it was impossible for her to see him any way other than sexy and appealing. One month of intimacy with him. The mere thought took her breath. His strong hands held the wheel and he watched the road, but she suspected he was aware of her gaze on him.

He was irresistible, yet at the same time he was another billionaire who lived by his own rules and thought of the world in relation to himself. She longed to fling her refusal at him, yet wisdom held her back. There was too much at stake to do that, and she knew she would eventually accept or hate herself forever; yet each time she was on the verge of saying yes, every principle in her screamed no. She admitted to herself it was his high-handed, presumptuous attitude that aggravated her.

As she studied his profile, she tried to think of any conceivable way to avoid accepting yet not lose what he had offered. She couldn't come up with any possibility. To get the money and sale, she had to become his mistress. Live with him starting immediately! She might as well accept his proposition, yet the prospect was dizzying. Her gaze ran down the length of him and desire was hot, intense. And could she possibly be his mistress for a month without having her heart shattered far worse than the hurt she had suffered from her broken engagement?

At the restaurant she barely noticed the linen-covered tables or heard the soft piano music in the background. In the flickering candlelight all she could see was her handsome escort who wanted her to be his mistress badly enough to make her a fabulous offer.

He smiled and reached across the table to take her hand. "You're worrying far too much. Let it go for tonight and enjoy the evening. Whatever your decision, it'll be easier to make. You'll know better whether or not you enjoy being with me."

"You and I both know already that I like going out with you," she replied, aware of his fingers rubbing her knuckles while his eyes conveyed his desire. "I wish you'd stayed that Montana cowboy you must once have been."

"Had I done that, you wouldn't be getting this offer, which should be advantageous for both of us, not just one. I won't be the only one to benefit from it," he reminded her, and she merely nodded.

They ordered dinners, and after the entrees arrived, Laurel ate only a few bites before putting down her fork. "I can't imagine eating one more bite of food. You say to let it go tonight, but how can I forget even one full minute the prospect of becoming your mistress or the financial offer you've made?"

"Dance with me and maybe moving around will get your mind off your decision." He raised her hand to brush his lips across her fingers, his warm breath sending another sizzle racing over her nerves. "You're beautiful, Laurel," he whispered.

"Thank you," she answered, pleased in spite of herself.

In his arms on the dance floor, Chase smiled at her. "So, tell me about growing up in Montana and where you went to school and what you did."

She tried to focus on answering his question and get her mind off his proposition for the time being. "We lived here in town most of the time so we could go to school here," she said, telling him about her early years. Chase was an attentive listener, adding tidbits about his boyhood, and soon she forgot for long moments the problem at hand as she laughed with Chase about their childhoods.

"I mentioned before that my dad was always ready for a party and always having groups of friends out to our place. He played the banjo and sang and taught all of us to sing and perform with him," she said.

"Do you play the banjo?"

"Heavens, no!" she exclaimed. "I learned to play the piano and to sing and dance, so I would sing while he played the banjo—we all sang."

"I can't imagine my dad cutting loose like that," Chase said. "He worked until he was exhausted every night. He was out working before sunrise and didn't come in until after sunset. There wasn't singing and dancing and we worked, too. I don't remember when I didn't work. Maybe that's why I like to play now," he stated, and she wondered about his life.

"Don't you want to settle sometime when you're older? That's a bleak outlook on life."

"Bleak? Far from it," he replied. "From my viewpoint, it's the best possible outlook."

"Are your parents unhappy in their marriage?"

"No, not as far as I know, although I certainly would be in the same situation. I've tried to give them trips, but they won't go. I don't ever want to be in that kind of relationship. Marriage looms like prison."

"I have an entirely different view," she said, realizing Chase was definitely a confirmed bachelor and still thinking it was a bleak outlook.

"We had parties, often several times a month, either in town or on the ranch in good weather. I grew up playing, but Mom saw to it that we worked, also," she said.

"Then I'm surprised you're not one of those party women. You've shouldered a lot of responsibility," he said, studying her as they danced.

Gazing into his eyes, she could see desire ignite in their depths and the moment changed. She forgot their conversation and became aware of their hands touching, their bodies pressed together lightly, and she wanted his kiss.

"Let's go back to the hotel," he suggested and she nodded.

The moment they were in the limousine, he pulled her into his arms to kiss her.

As they entered the hotel, the clerk handed a note to Laurel. Frightened, she feared any late call concerned her dad. "Chase, wait a minute," she said as she scanned the brief message swiftly. Her fears lifted when she saw it was from a family friend, and she pocketed the note. "No big deal. Sorry, but I worry about my dad, so I have to check any contact."

"Sure. No problem," Chase replied, holding her arm as they entered the elevator and rode to the top.

"Want to come in for a little while?" she asked.

"Of course," he answered in a deeper voice, and she knew they would take up with kisses where they had left off.

Inside, she turned to wrap her arms around his neck. His arms banded her and he held her to kiss her long and hard. When he raised his head, her heart pounded. She opened her eyes slowly to find him watching her with a hooded expression.

"You think about my offer, Laurel. I had a great time tonight with you," he added.

"I did with you," she confessed, although she felt a degree of reluctance to admit it to him. He had far too much self-assurance already. "I'll think about it all night," she whispered, wanting to pull him back to kiss some more, knowing she might as well give him an answer this moment.

"I'll take you to breakfast and we can talk," he said. "How's seven?"

"Fine," she said.

He gazed into her eyes and caressed her throat. "You're fantastic," he whispered, leaning down to brush her lips with his, another tormenting kiss that heightened her desire.

He turned and left, shutting the door behind him. Wanting to kiss him again, she stood motionless, her entire body tingling with awareness. She ran her hand across her forehead and walked in a daze to her bedroom. She knew there was only one answer to give him.

Agree to become his mistress and the hotel was sold. Half a million on top of it. For the first time she allowed herself to consider what his offer truly could mean to her and her family, and it made her weak in the knees.

She sat at her desk and noticed a blinking red light on her phone, which jogged her memory about the note she'd been given downstairs. She withdrew it again. *Need to talk to you tonight— Ty Carson.* She thought of the local rancher who had been a friend of her family all her life and was her best friend's father. She listened to her voice mail on the phone to hear a message from Ty asking her to return his call no matter what time she got the message.

The urgency of his calls puzzled her, and she picked up the phone and dialed the number he had left. After one ring he answered, said he was in the hotel bar and asked if she would meet him so they could talk.

With growing curiosity, she took the elevator to the first floor and saw Ty waiting near the door to the darkened bar.

With the sun-toughened skin of a Montana rancher, he was in jeans, a white shirt and a western broad-brimmed hat. He spotted her and headed toward her, meeting her with a brief hug.

"Thanks, Laurel. I know it's late, but this is urgent. Where can we talk?"

"Why don't we go to my office?" she said, leading the way. Instead of sitting behind her desk, she turned a chair to face him. He tossed his hat on a sofa by the door and raked his hand through his salt-and-pepper hair as he gazed at her with a solemn expression.

Placing his elbows on his knees, he leaned forward. "I wanted to see you about Chase Bennett and his outfit. Your dad is in the hospital and he can't talk to you, and I feel responsible to try to help in his place even though I'm not family, but I'm close. Your grandmother won't and your sisters aren't able to discuss this with you."

Becoming increasingly puzzled, she smiled uneasily. "Mr. Carson, you don't need to worry about me."

He held up his hand. "Just call me Ty, Laurel. I'm worried about you—me and my family and everyone else in these parts. If things were reversed, I'd feel better if your dad talked to Becca. By the way, she doesn't know I'm here."

"I appreciate your concern," Laurel said, thinking about Ty's eldest daughter.

"That man is coming in like a whirlwind and trying to change everything he can. A bunch of us are getting together to talk about what we can do to protect ourselves."

"Mr. Car—Ty, I'm shocked," she said, frowning. "I thought Chase's business here would help Athens."

"He's out for himself, not Athens. At the same time I'm worried about you. I've heard that he's taking you out, and I know you're getting over a broken engagement. The hotel is for sale, and I assume it's to help pay your dad's hospital expenses. Whatever the problems, Laurel, we all need to band together to help each other. The man is a shark, and he's after too much around here."

"I really appreciate your concern, but I'm fine and I can deal with him," she said, thinking about her evenings with Chase and his offer and realizing it had all become more complicated because local people must be viewing him as an enemy.

"Laurel, you can't deal with a man like this. He has endless resources. He wants my ranch and he's after it however he can get it."

"You absolutely don't care to sell?" she asked, surprised that Chase wanted the Carson ranch.

"Damn straight, I don't. My great-great-great-grandfather started our ranch, and it's been in the family since that time. What would I do, where would I move? And there's no good reason to sell. Oh, Bennett has offered a huge price, more than I could get if I put the ranch on the market, but that's no incentive. My boys like the ranch and I expect them to take over eventually."

"Why does Chase want it?" she asked. All her life, particularly as a child, she'd seen her father and his friends as strong, invincible men. Now her dad was in a coma in a hospital, and here was his friend, Ty, appearing older, worried and sounding vulnerable—it gave her heart a painful twist.

"My ranch is adjacent to the field he's discovered, and I have water—more abundantly than anywhere else—and my place would give him the easiest access from Athens. Let me show you," he said, reaching into his hip pocket and pulling out a folded, tattered paper. It had been torn out of a book and she saw it was a map of Montana. He had circled Athens, and beyond Athens Ty had drawn a red circle around his ranch. Beside his ranch, with a yellow marker, he'd circled the field where Chase would drill, and instantly she saw that the best access from Athens would be across Ty's ranch.

"Oh, heavens!" she exclaimed, looking over the map. The best town for him to center his activities in was Athens because other towns were farther away from his new oil field.

"He's pressuring me something fierce and thinks he can run me off my own land," Ty said.

"Well, in this day and time, he can't do that," she said, irritated again by Chase's selfish actions.

Ty shifted uncomfortably and scowled. "He can't run me off, but he can make life harder for me if I stay."

"How? I can't imagine he would do anything like that."

"He would in a flash. He's already bought the Higgens' place, and he can divert water that I get. He can boggle up a couple of entrances to my place where it's not as convenient for me to come and go. It's little things mostly—so far," he added darkly. "Bennett can buy up some of the local supply places and raise prices, which will hurt all of us. His people have made it clear that he's determined to get my ranch, and what's worse is there's a huge chunk of the ranch I took a loan against three years ago, and there are rumors that he's considering buying the bank. Mitch knows if he doesn't sell to him, Bennett will start his own bank here."

She shivered slightly with a cold chill. How

ruthless was Chase? How far would he go and how much would he hurt local people to get what he wanted?

"I just hoped to make it clear to you that we'll all give you assistance if you need help," Ty said and she nodded.

"Thanks. We're all right, and with Dad's health I do want to sell the hotel and the ranch. The doctors have told me that Dad may not be able to take care of any of it again the way he did. If we still own it all, he'll try."

"You can't know that for certain, Laurel. I think you ought to hang on until he recovers— a bunch of us are willing to try to help you. We'll support him, too."

"Thanks so much, Ty," she said, touched by his offer. "That means a lot, and I wish Dad could know what you're willing to do."

"The Durbins, the Malloys, the Dubinskis. I could keep giving you names—we're all banding together to protect each other from Bennett. I don't know whether we can because he is already putting too much pressure on us." Ty stood. "It's late and I need to get home. Molly worries when I'm gone. Stay away from Bennett, Laurel. Be careful. The guy doesn't have your interests at heart."

She walked to the door with Ty. "Thanks again," she said, patting his arm. "I'll think about what you've said. Please tell Molly and Becca hello."

"Sure. You be careful. Call anytime you want me. Don't let him pressure you, Laurel. And don't let him sweet-talk you, either. You know my cell number."

She nodded and watched him walk down the hall and turn the corner. Then she closed the door, leaning against it to think about what he'd said to her.

How ruthless *was* Chase? she wondered again. If she moved in with Chase, would townspeople be angry with her and feel as if she were siding with the enemy?

When she'd heard about the new discovery of the Montana field, she'd thought it would be a windfall for Athens and all the ranchers in the surrounding area. Evidently, some people would be hurt in all the change. Yet if she accepted Chase's offer, it would be a windfall for her.

She switched off the lights and went the back way to her floor. A light shone beneath Chase's door, and she wondered what he was doing. She went to her suite and stepped inside, moving automatically while she contemplated her choices.

Debating both sides, she pulled on a long nightgown and cotton robe and switched off lights, curling up in a chair to gaze outside into the darkness and consider Chase's proposition.

Two hours later she came to the same conclusion she had every time she considered various possibilities.

Tomorrow she would have breakfast with him, and she needed to give him an answer. If she waited much longer, he would seduce her anyway and his offer would be beside the point. Then she would lose not only the sale of the hotel but also the bonus of half a million dollars. Too, too much for her to turn down, and he knew it.

The next thing was to decide whether there were any concessions that she wanted to try to wring out of him.

After tossing and turning, Laurel woke early the next morning. Following her usual morning routine during summer, she slipped into her bathing suit and went down to the pool to swim. It was locked at that time of day, but she had a key. She placed her things on a chaise and dove into the cool water, swimming laps and trying to work off some energy and worries. Breathless, she bobbed up at the deep end, catching the side and tossing her head back to get water out of her eyes.

"Good morning," a deep voice said, startling her. Chase sat on the edge, his feet dangling in the water.

"You're not supposed to be out here!" she blurted. "How did you get in?"

"Bribery," he replied easily. "And now I'm glad I did. I like a morning swim. It gives me a chance to think. I suspect we share that."

While she was annoyed to find that an employee had been talked into letting him in early, her attention was taken by broad shoulders, a stomach like a washboard, with a well-sculpted chest and firm biceps. In spite of bobbing in cool water, heat ignited in her, spreading, playing havoc with her pulse. Dark curls were a mat across the center of his impressive chest. In his clothes he had looked good, but out of them he was breathtaking.

He dropped off the edge and bobbed in the water by her, placing his hands on her waist and lifting her slightly as he looked her over leisurely. When he did, the hot pink suit that she had pulled on so casually this morning suddenly seemed skimpy and revealing.

"We can skip breakfast," he suggested, his gaze returning to hers, and she knew what he was asking.

"No, we can't," she answered breathlessly. "You promised breakfast, and I'm holding you to it."

"I want to hold you to something else," he said in a deeper tone, and every nerve came alive. She twisted free and swam away, aware that he followed and kept up with her. At the shallow end she stood, water running off her. His gaze moved over her again in a slower, more thorough study down to her thighs.

He inhaled. "I think I better let you go in ahead of me," he said and flung himself into the water to swim away from her. She climbed out of the pool with her back tingling, sure he was watching her whether or not he was swimming. She scooped up her towel and headed to the gate. As she stepped through, she glanced back to find him standing on the side of the pool with his towel in his hand while he stared at her.

She turned swiftly but not before feeling another wave of heat in her lower regions. He was a magnificent hunk, making his offer even more tempting. She hurried the back way to her room and headed for the shower, unable to shed the images of him, too easily imagining him without that last scrap of clothing and knowing he was probably doing the same to her.

She bathed and dressed carefully, selecting an indigo cotton suit, a matching blouse and high-heeled matching pumps. She combed, looped and pinned her hair at the back of her head.

Promptly at seven he appeared, wearing a charcoal-colored suit with a fresh white shirt. He smiled as he looked at her and stepped inside.

"You're breathtaking. So far, this is starting out to be the best day I've had in Montana."

She laughed. "I know better than that!"

"Soon I hope I get to take down your hair," he said in a husky tone that added to her anticipation. He was more desirable each time she was with him—clean-shaven, hair combed, a scrubbed look about him. His aftershave was another enticing scent. He looked dressed for a photo shoot, which he could have done easily with great model potential. All that thick brown hair made her want to run her fingers through it, and she tried to keep her gaze away from his mouth. His heavily lashed, fascinating green eyes were doing enough damage to her self-restraint already.

He stepped closer to touch the corner of her mouth. "I like your smiles," he said. "Even though so far there haven't been many of them."

"These are not the happiest of times."

"I'm sorry to hear that, and I know it's because of your dad."

"My dad, selling the hotel, being away from my business—mostly Dad."

"Any chance you want to give me your decision this morning?"

She noticed that he watched her closely. She smiled again as she shook her head. "Let's wait until after breakfast and let me have a few more minutes of public time with you before we get down to business."

"Down to business—not really. This is something else."

"Down to lust?"

"Still something else," he said. "I like being with you. Lust can be easily satisfied."

"I guess I should be flattered," she said, still reluctant to give him her answer and knowing she was putting it off. She'd already resigned herself to what she was going to do. "I'm ready to go to breakfast," she said, gazing up at him and feeling as if he were on the verge of kissing her and beginning to want him to even though she was angry with him.

He crossed the room to hold the door and the moment was gone, but she was excited by merely thinking about his kisses. In the hall he took her arm, his fingers a faint pressure, yet she was conscious of it.

"An old family friend came to visit me last night after I left you. It was Ty Carson," she said.

"Wasn't that a little late for a friendly visit?" Chase asked. They entered the elevator and she saw speculation in his expression.

"He's worried and wanted to warn me about you. He said you're after his ranch, which he doesn't want to sell. His great-great-great-grandfather established that ranch, and Ty loves the place. He was raised there and his kids grew up there."

"I'll admit, I'd like to buy it. I've tried to make him an extremely good offer," Chase said, running his index finger along her collar and distracting her.

"He's adamant about it, Chase. He doesn't want to leave his ranch."

Chase shrugged. "That's his preference. Whatever he wants to do." The elevator doors opened, and she was quiet until they were seated and had ordered breakfast.

"Ty seems to think you'll force him to sell or make life unpleasant for him," she said, watching Chase, but he had no reaction to her statement. Seated across from her, he looked every inch the executive he was, as well as still looking as if he were ready to model. The man was handsome, but there was a cool look in his eyes that indicated the power he wielded. Already she was certain she would have to guard her heart well or he would break it far worse than any hurt inflicted by Edward.

"How on earth can I force him to sell?" Chase asked.

"I guess by making ranch life a little more difficult for him. He said something about limiting the availability of his water. He mentioned that you've already bought a ranch that borders his place."

"That doesn't have anything to do with him. It's a business deal," Chase replied in an off-handed manner.

"Ty's a good man, Chase," she said quietly. "I've known him all my life. I've known the whole family, and his daughter is my best friend. He said you want to buy the bank, too."

"I might," he replied with a faint smile, "but I think that also falls under business and shouldn't make me villain of the year. I really expect my company to help the town of Athens."

"I hope so," she said with sincerity. "One last note before I leave the subject of Ty's visit—he warned me to avoid you. By being seen with you, I may test friendships."

One of Chase's dark eyebrows arched. "I'll admit that's bad news, and I'll have to work on my image with the locals. I don't want to hurt you or cause you trouble."

She shrugged. "I'll worry about that. You don't need to. Just try to avoid riding roughshod over people or hurting someone needlessly," she added.

"I don't intend to, but there are things in work that have to be pursued—you're self-employed, so you should understand."

"I comprehend firm dealings and fairness and honesty, but I don't want to hurt anyone or take their home from them."

"You make me sound like Simon Legree," he said, smiling and leaning forward to touch her chin. "If the townspeople are getting down on me and want you to avoid me, perhaps we should spend our time together away from Athens."

She reached across the table to take his hand. "We'll keep a discreet distance when we're in public. Now, let's enjoy breakfast and then we can go talk in private."

Instantly his eyes darkened, and he inhaled. "Want to go now and have breakfast sent up?"

"Do you think we'd really eat? We have some wonderful strawberries that I've been drooling over."

"There's only one thing in this hotel that I'm drooling over, but I'll wait if I have to," he said, gazing intently at her.

"That's good. It's a glorious morning and I've had a refreshing swim and worked up an appetite."

He smiled and reached out to take her hand again. "I won't mention my appetite," he said, yet she knew what he wanted.

"You just did," she reminded him and they both smiled. Was he really the ruthless monster Ty had described? Would Chase help or hurt Athens? He expected to help the town and she couldn't imagine that he wouldn't, yet she worried about Ty almost as much as if he were part of her family.

The waiter came with their order and refilled sparkling goblets with orange juice before he left.

"Tell me about Athens and the people who live here," Chase said.

"Nearly everyone knows everyone else," she said. "Until my generation most people didn't move away and the town grew. But that's not true currently—most high school grads go to college, on to jobs and never return. I'm an example of that, and I don't expect my sisters to come back here to live. I don't care for ranch life—neither do my sisters. I think my grandmother is tired of dealing with the ranch, and I don't think any of them will mind moving to Dallas."

Chase asked her about specific people he had met, the local lawyers, various business people, until breakfast was finished and they left to go to her suite.

The one subject he didn't broach was his offer.

"I have an appointment at nine this morning, and sometime today I'm going to the hospital to see Dad," Laurel told him as they rode in the elevator. Her palms were damp because it was time to give him his answer and at this moment she could still change her mind. Was she making a decision she would regret deeply? Or one that would be a relief to her later when she looked back on it? With each minute tension coiled tighter in her.

Once inside her suite, he closed the door and

the lock automatically clicked, sounding loud in the silence.

He shed his coat, loosened his tie and strolled to her, placing his hands on her shoulders. "I think it's time I hear your decision on my offer. Will you be my mistress for the next month?"

Five

"**I** have a counteroffer," Laurel said quietly. "I don't know how much you'll bargain to get me to accept what you've proposed. I've been warned that I'll be hurt, that you're ruthless. Also, I think if I have a close relationship with you, folks around here are going to be unhappy with me. Therefore it has to be worth my while. And you are well able to afford more than you offered, and you know it."

Amusement lit Chase's eyes. "I can guess— you want more money."

"That's right," she replied, hoping he couldn't hear her pounding heart. "I want another quarter million on top of what you offered."

He nodded. "Fine. Do we have a deal?" he asked.

She realized she could have asked for a million and he probably would have agreed as swiftly. "Also," she added, her heartbeat racing as she tried to blank out what she was committing to. "There are two more things. I'd like to be able to continue to live in my suite until we move to Dallas."

"Certainly. I would have offered that anyway. I want you living here, hopefully closer than this suite. What else?"

She took a deep breath. "I can't imagine jumping into bed in the next few minutes. I want until tonight at least."

As he smiled, triumph sparkled in his eyes. "Excellent," he whispered. "You have a deal."

All the time she'd talked, an inner voice had screamed to avoid accepting, but she knew she couldn't. She had way too much to gain and not much to lose, if she could only remember to guard her heart. That would be the biggest danger to her well-being. She might be ostracized by locals, but she could weather their hostility and she would move back to Dallas eventually.

"Can you clear your books and go away for the weekend with me? Locals are getting hostile over how much I'm seeing you—actually over how much you're seeing me. Let's get out of here for a weekend. If anything changes with your dad, I'll fly you back immediately," Chase said.

"Where are we going?"

"I have a home on the California coast."

"Very well," she answered, knowing the chances of having to get to the hospital in a hurry seemed slim, but she didn't want to be too far away.

"Then we have a deal. I'll get my attorney working on the purchase this morning and we'll close as quickly as possible. I'll see if I can't have the closing moved up. We need to get the inspections done—the usual routine."

"It's a little difficult to accept that this is actually happening," she said, feeling stunned as she began to think about the sale and the money she would have.

"I'll put the money into an account for you today," he said.

"Since I'm going to be living with you, I want you to meet my family. Can you go to the ranch with me tonight?"

"Meet your family?" he asked with a frown. "This isn't a long-term arrangement," he reminded her. "If you take me home to meet the family, won't that be an implication that our re-lationship is serious?"

"Whether it is or not, if I go off for the weekend with you and then move in with you, I want them to know you," she said flatly, trying to retain her patience. "I don't want them to hear I'm seriously involved with you when they don't have a clue who you are."

"We're not going to be 'seriously' involved," he remarked dryly.

She bit her lip and her temper rose. "If I'm living with you for a month, I'm seriously involved, Chase."

"That's fine," he said, rubbing her upper arms, "but when the month is over, I'm gone."

"You've made that abundantly clear," she snapped.

"Why do I suspect your grandmother won't like me at all?"

"What do you care?" she retorted, surprised that he even brought up the subject. Or were some of his old Montana values still alive? Why was he so opposed to marriage? His parents were still together and she hadn't heard him say any dreadful thing about their relationship.

"I'm not worried," he replied in an unconcerned tone. "I'm surprised you wanted to introduce me to them. Your younger sisters will probably find the whole idea exciting that you've got a new man in your life so soon after Edward."

"I'm sure you're right. Also, I want you to meet them anyway, because even though the entire family has agreed it's for the best to sell the hotel and get the responsibility for it off my father's shoulders, this hotel is our heritage and has been in our family since the first Tolson settled in Montana. The sale is probably the most difficult for my grandmother. I'd like my family to meet you and get to know you a little so that won't seem so cold and impersonal."

Smiling, he rubbed his knuckles lightly on her cheek. "Softie. Sure, I don't mind. I'll be happy to meet them. I can't guarantee that they'll approve of whatever I do with the hotel."

"That's all right. In time, it won't matter so much. If they move from Montana, it won't be important at all."

"I remember your sisters are Ashley and Diana. What's your grandmother's name?"

"You have a good memory. It's Spring Tolson. I call her Gramma."

"Your sisters are seventeen and fifteen. It won't be long until Ashley will be going to college."

"Yes, and now I'll be able to send her."

He smiled at her. "Hopefully, you'll never regret your decision to accept my offer."

"Time will tell," she said, her thoughts on business at hand. "I'll call my real estate agent, inform Brice and let my family know. I'll tell them we'll get there about six. How's that? We'll have to leave here about half-past four."

"Fine," he replied, sliding his arm around her waist. "At last," he whispered. Her heartbeat quickened and her lips tingled in anticipation as she slipped her arms around his neck.

He kissed her possessively, and she returned his passion with her own. Fires built deep and low inside, and her hips arched against him, his arousal evident. His arm tightened around her waist, pulling her closer.

Thoughts spun away as her temperature soared and desire became torment. She ran her hands across his broad shoulders and felt his hands moving on her as he pushed away her suit jacket and it fell around her ankles.

Then his hands were in her hair, pins spilled out and blond locks tumbled around her face.

Her desire flared, hot and intense. Wanting him more each time they were together, she knew she soon would be able to let go of constraints, to touch and kiss him as much as she desired. Eagerly, she combed her fingers through his thick hair, then she slipped her hand down to caress his nape and the strong column of his neck while she arched against him. Above the roaring of her pulse, her moan was dim.

His hand cupped her bottom, crushing her against him. He shifted, his fingers twisting free her buttons and reaching beneath her blouse to shove away the flimsy lace and lightly rub her nipple.

Desire escalated and she wanted to toss aside waiting, but caution prevailed.

She pushed away. "Chase, not so fast. We both have appointments soon. Not yet," she said.

His eyes clouded with desire. "I want you," he said in a husky voice, looking at her mouth.

Her heart pounding, she stepped out of his embrace. "It's early morning, Chase, and we have so many things to do today."

He nodded, but his gaze stayed on her mouth

and then ran hotly over her, as tangible as if it were his hands caressing her. His dark hair was tangled, locks falling over his forehead, always reminding her of the biker she'd first met. His fresh, immaculate shirt was slightly rumpled, and his slacks bulged from their kisses.

Chase came closer, sliding his hand behind her head. "It will be amazing between us, Laurel. You'll see."

"Watch out, Chase. You might fall in love."

"I might fall in love, but I won't marry. When the month ends, so will our relationship."

Even though she knew he wouldn't wed, his words were cold and harsh and gave her a twist of pain along with stirring her anger.

"You've made it clear you're a bachelor for life because of your parents' dull marriage," she answered coolly, determined to avoid losing her heart to him but equally resolved that if she did, to never let him know or show it.

He picked up his suit coat and slipped into it, straightening his tie and putting himself back together so he looked as neat as he had when he'd arrived. "I'll call my attorneys and get everything started. The sooner we begin, the quicker everything will be done. Do you want to meet me at your bank to make this deposit today? You should call your bank president and make an appointment for us."

"If you want to wait, I'll do that right now."

"Sure, it'll save time," he replied and followed her through the suite to the bedroom, where she crossed the room to a desk and in minutes had an appointment set up for eleven.

When she replaced the receiver, she gazed at Chase. "None of this seems real."

"It will," he replied, reaching out to lightly caress her nape again. "I'm counting the hours," he whispered, leaning down to kiss her. Standing on tiptoe, she placed her hands on his chest and kissed him back. In minutes he raised his head.

Dazed, as usual, she looked up to find him watching her intently. He put his finger beneath her chin and tilted her face. "This is going to be a long day," he said. "You're making me wait, which is what I was trying to avoid."

"You're getting what you want, Chase. Everything is the way you wanted."

"Soon I'll get what I desire—you, Laurel. I want to kiss each sweet inch of you," he whispered, brushing another kiss across her lips. "I have to go," he said, striding toward the door.

Following, she watched him with mixed feelings until the door was closed behind him.

For the first time what she was acquiring from Chase and what it would mean to her and her family sunk in, and she wanted to jump in the air and shout with delight. She thought about what she would receive—almost one million dollars today! She would be able to do so much for her family. She thought about telling her grandmother, but the minute she announced she was leaving for the weekend with Chase, the questions would commence and she dreaded answering them.

The hotel was sold. This was a monumental date in the history of her family because the hotel would no longer belong to the Tolsons. The loans with the bank could be paid off fully. She felt as if a crushing weight had lifted from her shoulders.

No more pacing the floor until wee hours of the morning, wondering what they would do if the hotel didn't sell or if the medical bills kept climbing. No more worrying over how she would get the proper care for her father. So many problems that Chase's money would solve easily. Joy bubbled in her, and she relished the relief that buoyed her and made her want to laugh and dance and sing. Her father's debts would be totally eliminated. Maybe someday he would recover and know all was taken care of and he had no worries.

The one thing to aim for as a goal was to come out of this arrangement with her heart intact. She dashed to the phone to call Brice to ask him to meet her in her office, then rushed to grab her jacket and look in the mirror. Her blouse was wrinkled and her hair tumbled over her shoulders. She changed into a fresh white blouse, combed and pinned her hair up, yanked on her suit jacket and left.

By the time she reached her office, Brice was standing outside the door. "What's happened? Is your dad better?" he asked. "You look like you've had good news."

"It's not Dad, but the next best thing right now."

"You sold the hotel?" he asked, following her into the office.

She spun around, hugged him and stepped away. "Yes! Chase has bought the hotel. I made a deal with him, Brice."

He smiled. "Congratulations! I'm happy for you, Laurel. You deserve this. You've really earned it. You've worked harder than any of us."

"I don't know about that. I had a big personal stake," she said. "Thank you, though."

"It's fantastic!" he exclaimed. "We'll celebrate officially soon when it's convenient for you."

"I can't celebrate too much with Dad in the hospital, but I'm happy, Brice. Thanks for all your help on this. You're getting a bonus for your part."

"Thanks, beyond words. I have a feeling I had nothing to do with this sale," he added dryly. "I'm beginning to hear rumors from various places that some are less than happy with Chase Bennett's heavy-handed approach and his taking over everything he chooses, so I'm glad you got what you want."

"I'm happy, Brice. Be sure you always remember that."

He gave her a quizzical look and his eyebrows arched. "Did you get the price you wanted?"

"I got my asking price, plus a generous bonus."

"That sort of boggles the mind," he said, his eyes narrowing as he studied her. "He must have really wanted the hotel."

"He did," she answered smoothly, becoming uncomfortable with the turn in the conversation. "I have to let Lane know. I'm sure Chase's people will call him if they haven't already."

Her cell phone rung. "Speaking of our realtor—here's Lane Grigsby."

Brice walked away while she talked to Lane and agreed to an appointment to sign the contract.

"Chase's realtor had called Lane, and we're meeting this afternoon in Lane's office."

"Again, congratulations!"

"I'm taking Chase home to the ranch for dinner tonight so he can meet Gramma and the girls."

Brice frowned. "Is it getting that thick with you and Chase?"

She nodded. "I guess it is in a way. I simply wanted him to meet them."

"You've had dinner with him and been with him constantly since his arrival. Now you're taking him home to meet the family. Laurel, be careful. You just got over Edward."

She smiled. "It's not serious and I'm not engaged and I'm fine."

"This conversation is a complete turnaround. I was lectured you to be nice to the man and you despised him without ever seeing him. Now that's reversed. Maybe I shouldn't have urged you so much to be nice to him. Don't get that involved with Chase Bennett. Your dad isn't here. If he were, I'd keep quiet, but I don't want to see you hurt again."

"Brice, everyone wants to take care of me because Dad's in the hospital. He's let me take care of myself since Mom died. I'll be fine, and Chase Bennett isn't going to break my heart. Not at all. He's not the marrying kind, and I'm not ready for that either. Especially to a playboy. I've been there and done that—at least an engagement—and I don't want to do it again."

As he walked toward the door, Brice held up his hands. "Okay, okay. Don't take my head off. I merely don't want to see you hurt by a man who is well known as a womanizer. I've watched him pass through the lobby and every female in sight drools. And I promise you, he won't marry."

"I'm not going to get hurt."

"I'll see you later. If you need me, call," he said. As he left, she stared after him with an uncomfortable feeling, postponing telling him that she was going away for the weekend with Chase and wishing no one would ever know. But the whole town would learn about it soon.

She called her grandmother to tell her that she was bringing Chase to the ranch for dinner that night. Next, she spent over an hour taking care of hotel business. At twenty minutes before eleven, she left to go to the bank. Chase was waiting. He watched her cross the lobby, and her insides churned beneath his gaze. Nothing seemed real about the moment, including the huge sum of money he intended to deposit into her account. Self-conscious beneath his steady gaze, she was also aware of Chase; she could easily look at him for hours on end. He stood, one hand in a pocket, the other at his side, looking as if he owned the bank. It was also a shock to realize that soon she would be living with him.

For a panicky moment she realized she still could back out without complications. The money hadn't been put into her account, and her anger over his arrogance still simmered. Chase had a ruthless streak, and she thought of Ty's and Brice's warnings—both justified. She could turn around right now, walk out and her life would be her own. She halted, looking across the bank into Chase's eyes, and then he sauntered toward her.

He didn't hurry, crossing the room as if she weren't his destination, yet he never took his gaze from her. As she walked to meet him, her heart drummed.

And then he was only a few feet away. "Ready?" he asked, but she suspected he was aware of what she felt.

One last chance. She debated once more, angry with him for his expectations, that damnable certainty that he could get what he wanted one way or another. Yet, she knew he would. The money and what it could do for her family was too fantastic. And so was Chase. She nodded. "I'm ready."

"You don't have to look as if I have a gun at your back," he said.

She smiled and moved on and he walked beside her.

The slender, graying bank president, Mitch Anson, a longtime family friend, could barely contain his curiosity while he ushered them into his office and chatted briefly. He continually studied Laurel as if she'd worked some sort of magic spell on Chase who seemed relaxed, no more disturbed than if he'd been depositing a couple of hundred into her account.

Chase wrote a check to her and she stared at the figures that would forever change her and her family's lives. She glanced up to see him watching her intently, and then she looked back at the unbelievable sum that was becoming reality and would be all hers within minutes.

"This is hard to fathom," she said with amazement.

"It's yours now, a bonus for the hotel," Chase said, she assumed for the benefit of Mitch Anson.

"I can't really believe it." She endorsed the check and gave it to Mitch, who stared at it, blinked and then smiled broadly at her.

"You've received a generous payment," Mitch said, smiling at Chase. "Quite fabulous."

"I'll be moving some of it soon, Mr. Anson," she said.

"Of course. If we can help with investments or savings, you know we will," he told her.

They finished and walked out with Mitch accompanying them. He was cheerful and chatty with both of them and it took a short time to get away, but once they were alone, she turned to Chase.

"Talk will be all over town before I get back to the office."

"I assumed bankers were supposed to keep such things quiet," he said.

"Mitch is good about most secrets, but everyone will know about the sale of the hotel. Besides, I think Mitch still sees me as a kid."

"I can guarantee you that I don't," Chase remarked, and she smiled at him.

"You never knew me as a kid."

"I still wouldn't see you that way now. Let's go get lunch before we have to meet at the real estate office."

They bought sandwiches and took them to the park to sit beneath the shade of a large black walnut tree. As they sat on a bench and ate their sandwiches, she studied him, curious, but hesitant to pry into his personal life.

"Penny for your thoughts. You're very quiet all of a sudden," he said.

She debated whether to really tell him what was on her mind or not, deciding to go ahead. "I was wondering about you. You don't have to answer if you don't want. Have you ever been in love and had a broken heart?" she asked.

"Nope, that's easy to answer. Not unless you count when I had my heart broken in the sixth grade. I thought I'd never recover. Patsy Lou Jessup wouldn't meet me after school for pizza. I thought the world was going to end."

Laurel smiled. "Did you ever kiss her?"

"Oh, my, yes. Fabulous kisses, even with braces, but it wasn't meant to be and the next year she moved to Detroit. I've never seen her since."

"I wonder if she ever reads about you."

"I doubt if she remembers me. I don't think I made much of an impression on her."

"Hard to imagine," she said, and he grinned. He shed his suit coat, rolled his sleeves up and removed his tie.

"I take it you haven't made Mitch an offer on the bank yet."

"No. Actually, my staff is dealing with what we acquire in Montana. I'd just planned to come for a couple of days to look over everything, go see my folks for a few days and then fly back to Houston. I got sidetracked," he said, smiling at her. "As far as the bank is concerned, if I buy it, will that be another mark against me?"

She shook her head. "I don't care whether you purchase the bank or not. As long as you don't hurt people."

"I hope to do the opposite." He touched a lock of her hair that had come loose. "You put your hair up again. It looks nice, but I like it down."

"Sometimes you'll get what you want and sometimes you won't," she said.

"You don't care whether you please me or not, do you?"

"I'm not worrying about it, if that's what you mean. I don't recall any stipulation about pleasing you," she said and amusement sparkled in his eyes.

"I hope to try to keep you happy," he said. "You're different from other women I've known."

"I can well imagine," she said, "but you tell me. How am I different?"

"You're more direct, for one thing. I know where I stand with you. You're not as eager to keep me happy."

She shook her head. "Makes me wonder why you're interested in me."

"You're gorgeous and sexy and there's fire when we're together, more so when we kiss—"

"I get the picture," she interrupted. She folded up the papers. "It's time for me to get back to the office, and soon we'll meet to sign the contract on the hotel."

His hand closed on her wrist. "You almost stopped and walked out of the bank today, didn't you?" he asked.

She took a deep breath and tried to curb the annoyance that still simmered in her. "You're arrogant, self-willed and flamboyant," she said. "I had a moment there, but I had made my decision and I stuck by it."

"I can't seem to improve my image," he said, standing and taking papers from her. "Get your purse and c'mon. We'll walk back to the hotel."

"So, how do you see me?" she asked as they strolled back, curious about his perception of her.

"Independent, alluring, a chip on your shoulder—maybe from Edward."

She shrugged. "You're probably right, at least about being independent and having a chip on my shoulder. Alluring, I wouldn't know."

"Trust me, alluring fits."

"My grandmother is probably cooking a roast right now," Laurel said, shifting the topic of conversation.

"Sounds delicious," he said. "I'm looking forward to meeting her."

Suddenly they were back at the hotel. Since they were in public, she said a professional goodbye; then she left him to go to her room and make calls.

Chase had a meeting to attend regarding the property they needed to acquire in Athens.

During the meeting, he realized he had let his thoughts stray from business to Laurel. Wryly, he thought that was another first in his life—several of them now with her, but all were meaningless and easy to explain. He had never had his attention shift from business because he was thinking about the woman he would go out with that night.

She was stunning. He couldn't wait to make love to her and was sure that would end the restless nights and his daydreaming when his mind should be on business. With a start, he realized he was thinking about her again, and he tried to concentrate on what was being said, too aware of Luke's frowning scrutiny. He resisted the urge to glance at his watch and see how much longer before it was time to meet her. His anticipation was building by the minute, and it startled him to realize he'd never felt this strongly drawn to a woman before.

He tried to put aside thoughts of Laurel and concentrate on what Luke was saying.

As the hour approached to sign the contract, Laurel's nervousness grew. She thought she was past that earlier, but she was having butterflies much worse than the morning because this would change the lives of everyone in her family—the Tolson legacy.

Her stomach churned and she wished she hadn't eaten lunch. How would her grandmother take the news tonight? The hotel had always been part of their family since earliest days.

Glancing at her watch, she saw it was time to meet Chase for their appointment with the realtor. One more giant step in the next hour that would change her future forever.

Six

Laurel had been quiet in the car, on the way over, and now when they were alone in Lane Grigsby's office while he left for a moment, Chase reached across the table to tilt her face up and look into her eyes. "You look solemn."

"This is a big step."

"You can still say no," he informed her.

"I know I can, but I won't," she said, taking a deep breath and knowing she had to go ahead with what she and her grandmother had planned.

Lane returned along with Chase's realtor, Sam Kilean, and both attorneys. As Chase stood to shake hands with his realtor and his attorney, she greeted Wes Hindley, her attorney.

"Laurel, you know Sam," Chase said easily, and she shook hands again with the heavyset, brown-haired realtor.

Copies of the contract were handed out at a long conference table. Lane carefully went over the contract with them, and finally it was time to sign.

She stared at the blank line for the seller's signature, the place that would deed the hotel to Chase. A shiver ran down her spine. Once more, she knew she could still stop now, return the money deposited earlier and get out of all dealings with Chase. When she signed the contract, then she would be locked more tightly into a deal with him.

Trying to reassure herself that she was doing the right thing and following the course she and her grandmother had charted, she stared at the figures written in the contract.

She glanced up to find Chase watching her. Firming her lips, she looked down again and knew there was only one thing to do. Feeling as cold as if she were in a blizzard, she penned her signature with a shaking hand. She looked up again to meet his gaze, but this time she saw triumph, which increased her anger. Once more she tried to focus on the figures.

She went through the rest of the meeting in a fog.

As they returned to the hotel, Chase took her arm. "Let's go to my suite and have champagne to celebrate. It will be hours until I drive tonight, so I can have one drink. I get the feeling that you're less than happy with me over this transaction."

"You know how I feel and you know why. And I can't keep from thinking about how the hotel has been in our family for generations until today. As far as being unhappy with you, there's lust between us that doesn't have one thing to do with emotions."

"I intend to change that," he said, and she frowned.

"You want it all, Chase. My body you're getting. My heart—no. It's as locked away as yours is from me," she declared, remembering clearly his hurtful words...*in a month I'll be gone...*

He studied her with an unreadable expression, yet she was certain he wasn't pleased. He was accustomed to women fawning over him. He had known he wouldn't be getting that with her, and there was nothing in their agreement about how much she liked or approved of him. Or even that she had to cooperate with him. She intended to keep her part of the bargain to the extent that she had to. She knew lust would override her anger, but she had no intention of falling in love with him.

The minute he closed the door behind them in his suite, he tossed aside his coat, reached her in two long strides and pulled her into his arms, his gaze triumphant.

"Congratulations to both of us," he said. "We're each getting what we hoped for. I want you, Laurel," he declared in a raspy voice.

Her heart thudded and she stood quietly, more enveloped in anger than desire, yet when she saw the longing in his expression, her breath shortened. He pulled her closer, his gaze lowered to her mouth, and as usual she forgot why she was annoyed with him. He brushed her lips, a warm, slight contact that set her aflame.

"Damn you, Chase," she whispered with no anger. Losing all her fury, she wrapped her arms around his neck, raising her mouth to his, impatient for his kiss.

Each time they kissed, she wanted more of him. She pressed against his marvelous body, relishing the hard planes, aware of his readiness. This was the moment to let go and accept Chase fully, and she knew it was going to be easy to do. He tugged her blouse out of her skirt, but she was only dimly aware of his light touches. Her skirt fell away and then in minutes her blouse followed. She loosened the buttons on his shirt and pushed it off his shoulders, running her hands over his muscled chest and tangling her fingers in thick chest hair. He was strong, sculpted, filled with vitality, and she wanted to touch and kiss him.

When he held her away with his hands on her hips, she opened her eyes, dazzled as she looked at him. "Chase," she whispered, tugging lightly on his hips.

His gaze moved slowly and thoroughly over her. "You're gorgeous!" he said. He held her back. "We're going to wait to consummate what we feel. I want a special moment for you, something you'll remember. I want you to desire making love as much as I do," he whispered and every nerve in her body tingled. The depth of her craving surprised her, yet reason returned and she gathered her clothes to pull them on, aware of his watchful gaze and his arousal, indicating what his body clamored for.

He stepped close to tilt her head up and look into her eyes. "Lovemaking will be special between us, Laurel. I know it will."

"You're so certain about what you want," she whispered.

He kissed her hard briefly and then released her. "I'll be back in a couple of hours, and we can go to your ranch."

She watched him pick up his coat and tie and stride out of the room, with one last look at her.

Shaken, she stared after him. She simply melted with his touch. She didn't want to and planned not to, but it always happened. How would she survive with her heart intact after a month of his lovemaking? How could she have gotten entangled with two playboys who trampled her feelings?

And when did the month start? With the signing of the hotel contract or with the consummation of their agreement in bed? She suspected the latter, so it would probably begin tomorrow and last until the eighth of September.

With Edward there had never been the fiery attraction that she had with Chase. She hated to acknowledge it, but that set him apart and there was no way to crush a running undercurrent of excitement.

Two hours later Chase knocked. When she opened the door, his gaze traveled over her beige slacks and matching blouse in a thorough study. "You look luscious," he said.

"You don't look so bad yourself," she had to admit, knowing it was an understatement. Dressed in black slacks and a black knit shirt and hand-tooled western boots, he made her pulse race.

"There's one thing we can fix," he said, stepping closer and tugging loose the beige scarf that held her hair tied behind her head.

Her blond hair cascaded across her shoulders and he smiled. "Much better," he said softly. "Now we can go."

He stood close enough that she could detect his aftershave, and when she looked into his eyes, her heart fluttered. Desire was hot and intense and she wanted to kiss him, but she didn't.

In front of the hotel, a valet held the door to a sleek black sports car. While she climbed inside, Chase walked around to slide behind the wheel. As they turned into traffic, he glanced at her. "Your grandmother does know I'm coming, doesn't she?"

"Of course. I told her I had a new friend I wanted to bring home."

"That screams a serious relationship," he remarked.

"You and I know better, and eventually my family will know that you've gone out of my life and they'll forget you."

"I'm glad I don't have a damn delicate ego," he remarked. "You would constantly trample it into the dirt."

She smiled. "I have absolutely no fear of that. You're the most self-assured man I've ever known, and I've known some champions."

"Wealthy Edward. Who else?"

"Actually, my dad. He always had total confidence in himself. Another reason it seems such a change and shock to the family. Chase, tonight I'd rather leave the impression with my family that we're in love," she said, even though she was uneasy about the suggestion.

"I can accommodate you on that one," he said, reaching over to take her hand and place it on his knee.

"I talk to at least one of them every day, and usually on weekends they come into town to go to the hospital and we eat together, so I'll have to tell them I'm going away with you."

Looking mildly amused, he glanced at her. "You're definitely a family person. If you're in Dallas, do you keep in touch like that?"

"Not that much, but it's different when I'm here, and it's not the same with Dad in the hospital."

"I can see that. Sure, that's one for which I'll be more than happy to oblige. How far are you carrying this? You're not telling them we're talking marriage, are you?"

"Good heavens, no!" she exclaimed forcefully, and he laughed.

"I should've known better on that one," he said. "You're on, then."

"Thanks, I think," she replied, dreading taking him home to the family but feeling it necessary before she left town with him. Would he have balked if she had said she wanted to indicate marriage loomed? She didn't care. She was into this and trying to make the best of it, reminding herself constantly what she was getting out of it. Her financial worries had ended and her responsibilities had lightened. She had taken the burden off her dad for when he recovered, and she refused to consider the possibility that he wasn't going to recuperate.

"I have business in the morning and I can't get away from here until about two o'clock. How's that with you?" Chase asked.

"Fine," she said, unable to believe she was going away with him for Saturday and Sunday. "That will give me time to go to the hospital and take care of things at the hotel. Until we have the closing, I still feel responsible for the hotel."

"It'll take about two hours to fly to my place, so we'll arrive in late afternoon. Your cell phone won't work there, but I'll give you a phone number for my landline, and you can pass it on to everyone."

He raised her hand to drop light kisses on her knuckles. His warm breath was the barest hint of what was to come. "I can't wait until tomorrow, although you're not as excited about the weekend as I am. I'll try to change that," he added in a low voice.

"We have a deal, Chase."

As he looked back at the road, he smiled. "I don't usually strike out so completely with a woman. Particularly if we have some kind of chemistry between us, and you and I have almost spontaneous combustion."

"I don't think it's quite that fantastic," she remarked dryly, "and you know the old saying, 'You can't win them all.'"

"I hope you're not still seeing Edward when

you're with me," Chase said quietly and she shook her head.

"No. I'm seeing Chase Bennett. I'm influenced by my experience with Edward, but I know it's you."

"I'll have to keep working at this," he said.

"Don't make me a project," she told him and turned to watch the countryside, dreading taking him home but determined to do it nonetheless.

When they finally passed through the tall posts with the iron sign declaring the Tall T Ranch, her tension increased and she wondered what her grandmother would think.

Soon they could see the two-story wooden ranch house surrounded by tall pines and outbuildings and a large barn behind the house and garage.

"It's great, Laurel," Chase said. "Reminds me of my home, actually."

"Why do I get the feeling you're sizing up the place to decide whether you want to buy it?"

"I thought you'd already put it on the market."

"I have, but I plan to talk to Gramma tonight about keeping it. At the time I didn't want Dad to come home to so much responsibility, but now, with the money from you, I can afford to wait and include my father on the decision to sell or I can hire more people to help him run the place."

"Sounds like a good plan," Chase remarked.

"Tonight I want to get Gramma alone to discuss the ranch, because whatever we do, the girls will go along with our decision. They don't have much interest in the ranch at this point in their lives."

He nodded. "This place looks first-rate and it's spectacular countryside," he said, and she gazed at the mountains beyond the house.

"It's a pretty place and a successful ranch, but it takes a lot of work. Pull up in front and we'll go in that way. I'll get a lecture if I bring you through the kitchen the first time here."

He smiled and stopped in front, coming around to hold the door for her. Dressed in jeans and T-shirts, her sisters appeared on the porch, and her palms grew damp as she went up the steps with Chase's hand on her arm.

"Ashley, Diana, meet Chase Bennett," she said. "Chase, this is my sister Ashley," she said, turning to the seventeen-year-old, who was an inch taller and had her blond hair in a clip behind her head. Ashley smiled as she greeted Chase, and Laurel turned to the shorter honey-blonde. "And this is Diana."

After they said hello to Chase, she hugged them, then saw her grandmother approaching. "Gramma," she said as the woman stepped out on the porch, her cool blue eyes on Chase, "this is Chase Bennett. Chase, this is my grandmother, Spring Tolson."

Offering his hand, he greeted her with a friendly smile. "It's nice of you to have me for dinner tonight."

"We're always happy to meet Laurel's friends. Won't you come inside," she said, and Chase stepped up to hold the door for everyone as they all filed into the wide entrance hall.

Permeated by enticing smells of roasting meat and freshly baked bread from the kitchen, the hall looked comfortable with wooden benches along its walls. Paintings of western scenes decorated the walls, while potted plants stood on the polished maple plank floor. She wondered if it was similar inside to the ranch home he'd grown up in.

As they followed her grandmother, Chase draped his arm across Laurel's shoulders casually, a gesture Laurel was certain was noticed by all three family members.

Feeling as if she were entering a haven, she walked into the front living area that held upholstered furniture and heavy mahogany pieces, some from the time the house was built. A painting of wild horses hung above the broad mantel.

When they were seated and her grandmother had served wine, lemonade and hors d'oeuvres, Laurel glanced at her sisters and then her grandmother. "I wanted all of you to meet Chase because we've become friends, but also I want you to know him because he's bought the hotel."

"Wow!" Diana exclaimed, her eyes sparkling.

"Congratulations and, I suppose, thank you," Spring Tolson said, lifting a glass of lemonade to him. "Here's to the new owner of one of Montana's oldest hotels. I'll have to admit that I have a lump in my throat to see it pass from our family, but the time has come and I know it's for the best," she added.

Her words saddened Laurel because of what had happened to her father to bring all this about. She suspected her grandmother knew the sale was the best thing to do but was hiding how deep her hurt ran over losing the old hotel that was such a big part of their family history.

Smiling and looking relaxed, Chase raised his glass in return and then sipped. "I'm glad to have it because it'll be a great place for my employees and their families to stay, and it's in excellent condition right now."

"Chase is paying our full asking price," Laurel added and saw a faint smile curl her grandmother's mouth.

"Then I definitely need to say 'thank you,'" Spring added.

"I enjoyed learning its interesting history, with two gunfights transpiring in the original bar and the tables salvaged from that original structure," Chase said.

"The hotel has a long and varied history. For that matter, so does Athens," Spring said.

"I think my employees will enjoy Athens. I certainly do."

In minutes Chase seemed to have her family charmed, and even her grandmother was laughing at his anecdotes of growing up on another Montana ranch. Laurel felt a degree better, yet it was difficult to relax because she still had to tell her grandmother where to find her during the weekend.

As she'd expected, her younger sisters were dazzled, both all but drooling over Chase and hanging on his every word. It was her grandmother's keen blue eyes that made her nervous, but as the evening wore on and Chase proved to be as attentive a listener as he was a storyteller, she felt better about bringing him to meet her family. Even so, she was anxious to have the evening end.

After dinner he joined them in cleaning the kitchen, and she wondered when he'd last done any such work, if ever. Next, they played a word game. Between rounds they paused and Laurel left to help her grandmother serve homemade peach ice cream. In the kitchen she got out crystal bowls and faced her grandmother.

"Gramma, I wanted to talk to you without the girls. I'm making enough from the hotel sale that we can take the ranch off the market if we want to."

Her grandmother's eyes narrowed and she studied Laurel intently. "How much are you making from this sale, Laurel? You said he's paying your asking price."

"I asked for more and he's agreed to it," she said, feeling heat flood her cheeks and wishing her grandmother weren't quite so astute.

"Are you certain you're doing what you want to do?" Spring asked.

"Very. And this will give us the opportunity to

hang on to the ranch until Dad can give us his input on selling."

"Laurel, your father may not recover," Spring said, looking away and wiping her eyes.

Laurel stepped close to give her grandmother's hand a squeeze. "I'm planning on his recovery and so should you," she said firmly. "What about taking the ranch off the market?"

"If you're sure you want to, fine. We can always list it again. Lane shouldn't be too unhappy to lose the listing after selling the hotel."

"That's right. There's one more thing I wanted to tell you," Laurel said, taking a deep breath. "I'll be in northern California this weekend, and I'll leave you the number before I go."

Her grandmother turned to stare at her. "What are you doing in California?"

"I'm going with Chase," she said, feeling her face flush.

Spring studied her intently. "This is soon after Edward. Are you sure about what you're doing?"

"Yes, I am," she answered. "I wanted you to meet him and to know my plans."

"I like him better than Edward," Spring said, "but maybe I'm prejudiced because he's from

Montana and he's trying to help your father. I don't want to see you hurt again," she added, moving to Laurel to hug her and then stepping back. "I want you to be happy."

Laurel felt a pang because if her grandmother knew the truth, she would be protesting what Laurel was doing and would run Chase right off the ranch. Sooner or later it would be obvious that there was a windfall of money, and her grandmother was a shrewd woman who would put it all together eventually and be furious.

"I'm glad you brought him home for us to meet, and even though I'm sad about it in many ways, I know it's best to sell the hotel. The money will help your father, and now he won't have such a burden."

Laurel reached out to squeeze her grandmother's hand. "I feel so much better hearing you say all that," she said, thankful for her grandmother's supportive attitude.

"The ice cream will melt, Laurel. We better get it served, although your sisters are probably delighted to have Chase to themselves."

Laurel laughed as she dished out scoops of peach ice cream. "I'm sure they are and I don't know which one is happier about it."

"They approve of Chase and I know they like him better than Edward, too."

"That's obvious," Laurel answered with amusement. Both girls had fawned over Chase all evening, and she knew when they learned she was going away with him for the weekend, they would be filled with questions.

By eleven Laurel could tell that her grandmother was tiring, and it was time to leave. The girls followed them to the car and were still waving as they drove away, but her grandmother had already turned and gone back inside the house.

Chase reached over to take her hand. "Nice family. We could've accepted your grandmother's invitation and driven back early in the morning before daylight."

"No. I wanted to get back and we accomplished what I went for. It would simply have been a few more hours of my sisters fussing over you. You do have a definite effect on women—of all ages."

"Your grandmother wasn't dazzled, but she seemed to accept me."

"She accepted you and approved and told me she liked you better than Edward."

"I'm not sure that's a big plus. I think you're

the apple that doesn't fall far from the tree—you're like her. I suspect if you'd turned everything over to her, she could have stepped in and run it all the way you have."

"You're right and she has in the past. She's running the ranch right now."

"You have a nice family. Be thankful your dad knew how to enjoy life. I take it you talked to her about keeping the ranch."

"Yes, I did and she agreed, so I'll call our realtor in the morning and take it off the market," she said, watching Chase. "I hope you've decided to back off on Ty's property."

"Actually, I haven't. I doubled my price and offered to let him keep his house plus ninety acres. That's a generous offer."

"I don't think it matters what you offer," she said. "He doesn't want to sell."

"He wouldn't have to move or stop ranching there. Every man has a price."

For the first time in the evening her anger toward Chase surfaced. Another glimpse of the arrogant, affluent man, she thought. "For his sake, I hope it's a deal he will accept because I know you won't stop until you get what you want. I've looked at the map and I saw why you want it. What I don't understand is why you're in such a hurry about all this, Chase? You'd think you'd sunk every nickel you own into developing this new field and have to have results immediately. But then, I don't really know you. Maybe that's the way you work."

He chuckled and caressed her knee, pulling up the leg of her silk slacks until his hand was on her bare skin while he kept his gaze on the road. "It's because of a bet."

Surprised, she turned to stare at him. "What on earth does a bet have to do with it?"

"A lot. I told you my mother has sisters. They were Texans and when they were in college, each of them married northern men. Mom married my dad, a Montana rancher, and moved here. Aunt Mercedes married a rancher from South Dakota and moved there. Aunt Faith married a man in the drilling business and moved to Wyoming. I've grown up seeing my cousins, Jared Dalton and Matt Rome, often and we're close friends."

"That's really nice, Chase," she said, having difficulty seeing him as caring about anyone else except himself. "I'm surprised. You seem so self-contained."

"We went to different colleges, but all were in Texas and we played football, so we competed and saw a lot of each other those years. Financially, we've all done well, and we get together once a year in Texas for a weekend-long poker game. After the last one in April, we made a bet. Whichever one of us can make the most money in the next twelve months wins. We each put in five million, so the winner gets his five back, plus ten million from the other two. In addition, the winner treats the others to a weekend."

"Good heavens!" she exclaimed, stunned by the high stakes and the reason for his rush. Again, all she could see was a wealthy, frivolous playboy. "This is because of a bet! That's an enormous amount!" she exclaimed, aghast.

"Don't look as if I'd just admitted to robbing banks! It's only a bet with my cousins. I don't gamble otherwise." He grinned. "It adds spice to life. So, I'm interested in getting that field developed and bringing in a profit as quickly as I can. Right now, the only thing I'm doing is spending money, but all of it is an investment that I expect will pay off royally."

"I'm sure it will," she said, wondering about the kind of high-stakes life he led, suddenly feeling as if she had discovered a chasm between their lifestyles. How could she ever have any common ground with him? She thought about Chase playing the word game with her grandmother and sisters. What a dull life he must think she lived.

"Where are your cousins now?" she asked after a period of silence.

"Jared works in Dallas and Matt headquarters in Wyoming and has several homes. Actually we all have homes in various places."

"You're trying to make the most money, yet you paid me a fortune."

He smiled again. "Not really," he said quietly, and she realized she could have easily gotten more from him, that he viewed what he was paying her as a paltry sum.

"That's decadent," she said, thinking he had two sides, the charmer and the arrogant mogul.

"Don't get in a huff over my money," he said with amusement lacing his voice. "It's doing us both good."

Clamping her lips together, she turned to stare into the darkness beyond the highway. At night, out of the city lights, she could see myriad twinkling stars, a sight rarely seen in town. Chase's life was far different from her own, yet he had the same kind of background, so they had similarities.

Tomorrow she would leave with him. Could she weather the weekend with her heart intact? She knew she'd better because she had the whole month to go.

He reached over to caress her nape, his fingers warm and light, causing tingles and making her want to touch him in return. "Tomorrow night at this time, you'll be in my arms," he said, and she knew that's what he was envisioning, while she was deliberately avoiding speculating about it.

Finally they arrived back at the hotel and at her door she turned to him. "It's late—actually early in the morning. I won't ask you in tonight and our month can start tomorrow night."

"I'm not rushing you now," he said in a thick tone that always indicated he was having erotic thoughts. "Until tomorrow night," he whispered and took her into his arms to kiss her. His kiss lengthened as she returned it passionately.

She was tempted to ask him in and start the month tonight, but she wanted to wait until they were away from the hotel to commence this re-lationship. Finally she pushed against his chest and he released her.

"I need to go in," she said breathlessly. "I'll see you tomorrow. Actually, in a few hours."

"Thanks for tonight, Laurel," he said solemnly. "I'll see you in the morning."

Nodding, she turned and entered her suite, leaning against the door and closing her eyes, relieved she didn't have to invite him in tonight yet wanting to at the same time. She ached for more kisses and was too aware of how badly she wanted him right now.

Feeling exhausted by all the events of the day, she thought she'd fall asleep instantly, but she tossed and turned most of the night, dreaming of Chase.

Saturday morning, as she dressed in a tailored white shirt and a straight, blue cotton skirt, slipping on high-heeled sandals, she thought about all the things she had to do before she left with Chase. The most onerous chore was to talk to Brice.

She had managed to deal with her family. Now she dreaded telling Brice about leaving for the weekend with Chase because Brice would know she wasn't the least bit in love with Chase.

She didn't get an opportunity to talk to Brice until after ten o'clock, when she called and asked him if he would come to her office. Seated behind her desk, she thought about Chase moving into her office soon.

She heard a light tap at the door and Brice appeared, smiling at her. Clean-shaven and dressed in a tan suit, he looked refreshed and energetic and brimful of his usual optimism. His blue eyes held curiosity.

"You wanted to see me?" he asked.

"Yes. Close the door and have a seat."

"This sounds serious," he said, sitting across from her, waiting expectantly with a faint smile still on his face. "What's up?"

"I guess in a way it's sort of serious," she said. "I'm taking the weekend off."

He shrugged. "I'd say that's good news because you've earned it. You've worked like crazy getting this hotel ready to sell and dealing with Bennett and his entourage. You've gone daily to see your dad, and if you're where we can reach you—and I'm sure you will be or you wouldn't be telling me this—we can get you back here soon if it becomes necessary."

"I want you to promise to call me if there's the least little reason that I should return."

"Sure, I will. You know that," he said and his smile faded as he studied her with curiosity.

"The girls will go see Dad tomorrow and Sunday, so they'll be around."

"There you go. You're not needed here. The hotel should be fine."

"Thanks, Brice," she said, wishing she could let it go at that, but she knew he would find out anyway from Chase's employees.

"My cell phone won't work. I'll have my Black-Berry and I can give you a landline number to call."

"Sure. I hope you have a great time. So, where exactly are you going?" The question hung in the air.

"I'm going with Chase to the northern coast of California."

All the blood drained from Brice's face and then flooded back, and he turned so red that she was frightened he might have a heart attack. "Brice—"

"Dammit to hell," he said quietly, clenching his fists. "This is why the hotel sold like lightning, isn't it? It's none of my business what you do, but if your dad were well, none of this would be happening."

"Not you, too!" she exclaimed. "Stop trying to

protect me because my dad is in the hospital. I've been on my own a long time now."

"Dammit," he repeated. "If your dad were well, you wouldn't have sold the hotel and you wouldn't be going away with that bastard. You traded the hotel for the weekend," he said bitterly and jumped to his feet to jam his hands into his pockets and pace.

She stood, unable to sit still either. "Brice, it isn't that bad."

"The hell it isn't!" he exclaimed, spinning around. "I've known you since you were three years old. I should've guessed he didn't fly in here and buy the hotel as easily as it appeared. I should've prevented this."

"No, you shouldn't have," she said firmly. "First, I'm an adult. Second, I gave it thought. Third, I'm doing what I want to do. I guess I can add a fourth—he has more than made it worth my while. He's not repulsive, either, Brice. We get along."

"He's Edward all over again only a lot worse. Dammit, I hate this. And I know there's nothing I can say or do to change things now. The hotel sale contract has been signed."

"I don't want to back out of the deal. Brice,

besides the sale of the hotel, he paid me personally three-quarters of a million dollars," she said quietly. Brice spun around to stare at her, his jaw dropping.

"Three-quarters of a million plus buying the hotel in exchange for a weekend?"

"A little more time than a weekend. And remember, he's a charmer and I enjoy being with him."

Brice combed his fingers through his hair. "How much more time?"

"One month."

He closed his eyes and rocked back on his heels. "I should have stopped this from happening. Ty talked to me the other night and said if Bennett gives you any trouble to let him know, that he felt terrible with you having to deal with Chase Bennett without your dad around."

"Ty Carson talked to you about me? I think there are some old-fashioned attitudes here," she remarked, feeling less defensive and slightly exasperated. "I did what I wanted to do. A month with Chase is not an unpleasant prospect."

Brice studied her intently and she gazed back at him as steadily. "He'll break your heart the way Edward did," Brice said finally.

"No, he won't," she replied firmly, aware she had recovered rapidly from Edward.

"I shouldn't have let this happen. The whole town will be talking about it and speculating."

"The whole town won't know that it's anything other than I've fallen in love with Chase on the rebound."

"I think you'll hear from Ty."

"I won't unless you tell him some of this. I wish, for my sake, you would keep the conversation we've had confidential."

"I damn sure will if you want me to, but people will talk and it'll get around that you two are together. You know that."

She shrugged. "Yes, I do, but that's okay. I've grown up with that going on in this town," she said, glancing at her watch. "There's constantly gossip about someone or something."

He gazed at her. "I feel as if I really let you down."

Walking closer to pat his shoulder, she smiled. "I'm fine, Brice. Now, please don't worry. It's time for you to meet with one of the inspectors."

"I should've done something," he repeated as he walked beside her. He opened the door and Chase was striding toward them.

Brice glowered at him and moved so swiftly that she didn't realize what was happening as he threw a punch and struck Chase.

Seven

Chase staggered back into the wall, and pain shot through his jaw. He stared at Brice in surprise, not having any idea what had brought on the rage.

"What was that for?" he asked, getting out a snowy handkerchief to dab at a cut on his cheek.

"You're bleeding! Brice, for heaven's sake, apologize!" Laurel exclaimed, as she stared at her employee.

Brice clamped his jaw closed and looked at Laurel and then back at Chase; Chase guessed what had Brice hot under the collar. Chase waved his hand. "Forget it. No hard feelings on my part," Chase said.

"Brice, please," Laurel pleaded, hanging on to

Brice's arm as if she feared he would attack Chase again.

"Sorry, Laurel, if I've upset you," Brice said to her, clearly indicating that the only person who would receive an apology would be Laurel. Scowling, Brice spun on his heel and stomped away.

She moved to Chase to take him by the arm. She smelled delectable, like flowers. "Your cheek is bleeding. Come into my office and let me give you something to put on it," she urged, and he was happy to go with her, wanting to pull her into his arms.

She closed the door behind them and Chase said, "I didn't see that coming until he was in my face. I take it you told him about going away for the weekend with me," he added dryly.

"Yes, that was why," she admitted, looking worried and biting her lip. "I assured him that I was doing what I wanted to do, that I enjoy being with you."

Chase shook his head. "I'll be a little more alert around here. Anyone else going to take a swing at me over taking you away with me?"

She took a deep breath. He tilted his head and stared at her because she hesitated before she answered. "I don't think anyone else will resort to violence, but I never would have thought that about Brice."

"Who else? You do think so or you would have answered instantly. Is it Ty Carson?" Chase asked as he followed her into the bathroom adjoining her office. She reached into a cabinet and withdrew a bottle, then fished out cotton and a gauze pad.

"I don't need all that," he said, wanting to chuck all the first aid and pull her into his arms. "Just let me get the blood off," Chase said, retrieving a washcloth to run water on it and dab at his cut. "Is it Ty?" he repeated, naming the most likely person.

"I don't think he would get in a fight with you, but I'm shocked that Brice did. And I know Ty is unhappy with you. Let me clean that cut the right way," she added, taking the washcloth from him.

She dabbed at his cheek, and Chase rested his hands on her waist as he inhaled her perfume and admired her clear, flawless skin. When she reached up to touch his cheek, the vee of her blouse revealed enticing curves.

"I'll have my guard up around the local men. Jealousy, I can understand. This came out of the blue. You aren't being forced to go away with me," he said, thinking more about undressing her tonight and wishing the hours would go faster until he could have her all to himself.

"That's what I told Brice," she said quietly, putting down the washcloth. "There. That should do. I'm sorry, Chase."

Feeling foolish, he grinned. "Brice caught me totally off guard. I was getting ready to shake his hand." He watched her. "You could kiss it and make it well."

She shook her head. "I'm glad you're making light of it. You won't hold it against Brice, will you? He's wonderful about managing the hotel."

"I won't do anything to cause him the least bit of trouble," Chase answered, not caring whether Brice ran the hotel or not. His staff would make those decisions, yet for a time he would pass the word to leave Brice where he was because if they removed him, Laurel would think Chase was doing it to get back at the man.

"I have an appointment in twenty minutes," he said, glancing at his watch, "and I'll be busy until we leave at two o'clock, but I wanted to see you."

"Well, we've finished cleaning you up. Let's get out of here," she said.

He followed her back into her office, then pulled her into his embrace for a kiss that grew steamier until her phone rang and he had to release her.

On fire with wanting her, he watched her as she hurried to her desk and bent over to grab the phone. Mentally undressing her, he perused the length of her and her trim backside and long legs, and his arousal responded to his erotic thoughts. She was reluctant to go to California with him, almost backing out of signing over the hotel yesterday, dreading last night. He intended to seduce her tonight, to wipe out every shred of reluctance until she was as wildly passionate as possible.

She was hot and tempting, and he was going to enjoy this month beyond measure. He suspected there would be tears and anger at the end of the thirty days, but she knew full well what to expect and he would be gone quickly. No woman had ever held him longer than he'd planned and Laurel wasn't going to either. Thoughts of the dull routine of marriage always loomed as a prison. He wanted no part of it. Yet how he wanted her! His nights were a torment because of dreaming about her and during his waking moments, thinking about her. Chase walked up behind her and ran his hand up her bare leg beneath the cool cotton material of her skirt.

She felt fabulous with her smooth, silky skin, good muscle tone, and shapely long, long legs. He wanted to be on top of her, both of them bare, his hands all over her, and by night that's what he expected.

She turned to glare at him and stepped away. He smiled, leaning forward to trail light kisses across her nape.

The tone of her voice thickened, her breathing became erratic and she gave him another glare. He knew he was distracting her, but she was talking about a food order for the hotel and he didn't care. He wanted to touch her in the few short minutes he had left before his meeting.

Finally she finished the call and spun around with fire in her eyes. "Chase, for heaven's sake! I was making a business—"

He stepped closer, wrapped his arms around her and kissed her, silencing her lecture. His tongue thrust into her mouth; there was a moment when she was still and unresponsive, but then her arms wrapped around his neck. Her hips pressed against him. She kissed him back with passion and fire and he groaned, knowing he had to stop and cool down for his business meeting, but she was too tempting.

Finally he released her and she opened her eyes slowly. Her full lips were redder, parted, and she looked up at him with a dazed expression.

"You make me want to chuck this meeting, but it's important. We're trying to make arrangements to use a trucking firm that's located north of here, and the owners are coming to talk to me. As much as I hate it, I have to run," he said, heading toward the door. "I'm late right now. See you at two, darlin'," he flung over his shoulder.

Outside her office, Chase began to cool down. He thought about the night before and her family who had been nice, yet it had made him nervous because he usually didn't get taken home to meet the family of his mistresses. All evening her grandmother had given him cool, assessing looks, and he suspected she was a shrewd woman who was sizing him up. It was done and over and he'd never see them again, unless he bought the family ranch, which he didn't expect to do.

That family visit was a first with her, and tonight would be another first. He kept his California home solely for a getaway for himself, and he'd never taken a woman there before. With her father in the hospital in the shape he was in, Chase knew he'd never get her to go too far from Montana, so the California house seemed best. And it was a good escape from hostile locals. He had never wanted to take a woman there before, yet he looked forward to having Laurel with him, which made him surprised at himself and his own reactions.

In so many ways she was the kind of woman he had always avoided—tied to family and old-fashioned values, aimed for marriage and children. She was too independent, too self-willed and too much of a take-charge person to suit him, one of those capable women who were probably descendants of the pioneer stock that settled Montana and could endure all sorts of hardships and manage well. He preferred a so-phisticated, uncomplicated beauty whose biggest worry was her pedicure and hairdo. Yet Laurel was incredibly beautiful and luscious. She took his breath away, and his body reacted swiftly to her slightest touch or the rare moments when she flirted with him.

He rushed into the meeting room to find only Luke. "The others have been delayed by a tie-up in traffic on the highway. They'll be here in about ten minutes," Luke said, his gray eyes assessing Chase.

"Damn, I didn't have to hurry after all," Chase said.

"I wanted a moment with you. We've set a closing date for the hotel for the fourth of September.

"Fine. That should suit Laurel, too."

Luke eyed him. "What happened to your cheek?"

"Brice threw a punch."

"I'll be damned. Doesn't he know you're his new boss?"

"He doesn't care. There's a streak of independence in people around here. Must be something in the Montana air," Chase remarked lightly.

Luke's scowl grew. "That isn't funny. Why did he hit you? Let me guess—it's over Laurel Tolson and you. Brice must have found out you're taking her away with you tonight."

"She told him. I didn't even see it coming.

They stepped out of her office as I walked up, and next thing I knew, I'd been hit. I never expected it."

"You went home with her last night, and then one of her employees slugs you today. This isn't your type of woman, and she isn't one for you to fool around with, Chase. She isn't the love-'em-and-leave-'em type you like that has the same attitude about relationships as you. This one practically has a bridal bouquet in her hand."

"She knows I'm not the marrying kind. I've made that abundantly clear."

"You're getting her on the rebound from Edward Varnum. Frankly, I don't know how you talked her into going with you except you probably won her over by buying this ancient hotel for an exorbitant price. Let me introduce you to someone else."

"No. Don't bother bringing it up again. Thanks for the kind advice," Chase said, "but I'm doing what I damn well please and the lady is spending the weekend with me."

"You're taking her to California. Is there special significance in that?"

"Only that she won't go far away with her father in the hospital."

"Ah," Luke said, still frowning. Chase tried to hang on to his patience because besides being a valued employee, Luke was his friend and he knew that he meant well.

"Stop worrying. She'll be in my life awhile, and then she'll be gone and there will be another woman."

"I suppose. It's just that she's a ravishing babe and she's different, and you're doing things you've never done before with anyone else."

"Babe? That description doesn't exactly fit Laurel, but ravishing does. And there's no particular significance to what we're doing. I told you why we're going to California. She wanted her grandmother to meet the man who bought the hotel. No great meaning in that either."

"Did you have a good time last night?"

"I know you're asking that to see if you can discern something special in my visit with her grandmother, but there wasn't," Chase replied, struggling not to lose his temper. "Sure I had a good time. Grandma can cook beyond belief—too bad you can't hire her, although the chef here is damn good."

"That's the truth! I've already gained four pounds since I started staying here."

"Don't worry, I won't fall in love with Laurel and she knows this is temporary."

"Women like that never know a relationship is temporary. They always think they're different."

"Listen, Dad," he joked, "you're so damn full of advice, let me give you a clue—I can take care of myself where women are concerned. End of conversation."

"Sure, sure. On the business side, we gave your offer to Ty Carson about keeping his house and ninety acres and doubling the price, and he said no deal, but we told him to think about it and give us an answer in two days."

"Dammit," Chase swore, touching his sore cheek. "Stubborn old codger. Driving from Athens across his ranch to the oil field is the easiest and shortest way, and this town is the most convenient for me to use for a headquarters." Chase rubbed his forehead and thought about Laurel telling him about Ty; he knew that if he pressured Ty too much, she would be furious. He clamped his mouth closed and tried to think about how to get Ty Carson off his land. "Money doesn't tempt him, but there must be something. I want that damned ranch of his and we could use the water."

"He's stubborn as hell. I've talked to him twice now."

"Ty Carson may be the next one who'll try to slug me over Laurel. He's known her all her life, is the father of her best friend and is protective of her."

"Oh, hell," Luke said, looking glum. "I still say that she's not the best woman for you."

"Luke—" Chase said, a warning note in his tone.

Someone rapped on the door. Three men in suits poured into the room, and Chase smoothed his shirt and raked his fingers through his hair as he turned to greet them, trying to get his mind on business.

Halfway through their meeting, Chase realized someone was speaking to him and his thoughts had wandered. He tried to cover for it and didn't look at Luke. The men didn't know him and seemed unaware of his hesitation and switch in topic, but Chase knew Luke had noticed and hoped he didn't hear about it later because it wasn't the first time his mind had wandered.

Ten minutes later he found himself surreptitiously glancing at his watch. Time was dragging and it was still only eleven-thirty. He wanted out of this meeting and to finish his other business. Two o'clock couldn't come soon enough.

Laurel finished the hotel chores by half-past eleven and intended to leave for the hospital. She stopped by Brice's office to give him the phone number where she could be reached. He looked up, his features impassive as he stood, closed the door and faced her.

"Brice, please don't worry about me."

"I'm sorry if I caused you grief this morning, Laurel. I was so damn mad at Chase Bennett. I don't want to see you hurt, and I know you're doing all this for your family. If you didn't have any family, you wouldn't be going away with him."

"I do have family, so I've never even looked at it in that way," she said gently. "I can't."

"That makes it all the worse."

"I don't *have* to go."

"Oh, hell. Who could turn down almost a million on top of selling the hotel at a price you never dreamed you'd get? Lane is ecstatic and celebrating like crazy."

"I'm not surprised and I'm glad, because I had to tell him that I've taken the ranch off the market."

Brice frowned. "I thought you wanted your family to be free of the responsibility."

"It's different now," she said gently. "I can hire all sorts of people to run it and none of us have to deal with the problems, yet we can keep it— at least until Dad can make a decision about it."

Brice's scowl grew and he rubbed his jaw. "I guess it's good that you can take the ranch off the market. By the way, I've accepted a job with the Barclay Champion Hotel. I won't start until Bennett's outfit takes over here and you don't need me."

"Oh, Brice!" she exclaimed, hating to hear he was leaving the Tolson. "I know you have my best interests in mind and I appreciate that. I'm sorry to see you go, because you've been great. I think Chase will want to keep you."

"Maybe he'll offer me a million dollar bonus to stay," Brice stated with sarcasm, and she had to smile as she shook her head.

"I'm sorry it worked out this way. I felt better about leaving the hotel in your hands."

"You're leaving it in Chase Bennett's clutches. It's for the best for me to move on. I won't work for him and I'm sure the animosity is mutual. I'll be even angrier if he hurts you."

"That's sweet, and I appreciate your concern." She glanced at her watch. "I need to go to the hospital, and then I'll come back and leave at two with Chase."

"You take care of yourself and don't fall in love with him. This one won't offer you an engagement ring."

"He's made that more than clear, but I don't want one from him, either," she said quietly. "I really haven't changed my feelings about wealthy playboys."

Brice clamped his jaw closed and clenched his fists; she hugged him lightly and he patted her back in return. "I feel as if I've failed your dad and you. You take good care of yourself," he repeated.

"Stop worrying. I'll be back Sunday night."

"Sure. Call me if you want me to come get you."

She laughed and nodded. "Will you stop worrying, please!" she repeated and turned to go, still hurting that he was leaving the hotel yet warmed by his concern for her welfare.

At the hospital, she sat beside her dad and talked quietly, telling him about the sale of the hotel, Brice's leaving and taking the ranch off the market. Finally she kissed his cheek, chatted with their private nurse and left, catching the doctor in the hall and talking briefly. There was no change.

When she returned to the hotel, she packed a few things and looked through her clothing, trying to select what she wanted to wear tonight.

Opening a wide drawer, she gazed at her undergarments, wondering whether she wanted to look seductive to turn him on or look cool and aloof and remind him that her heart was not in this endeavor. Either way she expected to make love with Chase as soon as they were at his house.

She eventually selected pristine white lacy underwear and a matching bra, deciding she would go for cool and remote, but suspecting she could wear a tent over her head and it wouldn't cool Chase. Gathering her belongings, she went to take a shower.

At ten minutes before two she was ready with her bag by the door. Five minutes later there was a knock. Opening the door, she drew a deep breath. Wickedly handsome, Chase was in chinos, a white shirt, a navy sport coat and snakeskin boots. A black Stetson hat shaded his face. Adding to her pleasure at seeing him, she noticed how his gaze warmed with appreciation when he looked at her red silk blouse and matching slacks. She had let her hair fall loose, which she knew pleased him.

"You're beautiful," he said in a husky tone.

"Thank you and likewise to you," she replied, smiling. "Incredibly handsome."

He caressed her nape, then shouldered her bag. "I'd like to delay leaving a few more minutes, but I won't. The sooner we go, the quicker we'll be there—and I'll admit, I can't wait to get you to myself."

"Aren't you taking anything?" she asked as they stepped into the elevator.

"I've already had my carry-on picked up."

Her anticipation climbed because she knew they would make love when they arrived at their destination. They were driven in a black limo to his waiting plane and then flown to his home in California, where he had a runway and hangar on his land. When a car met them, Chase slid behind the wheel to drive them the short distance to his house. For the entire trip Chase was being his most charming, and she bubbled with excitement, which she knew she couldn't bank. For this weekend—and in many ways for the next month—she had to let go of her anger toward him and her resentment that he was another strong-willed man who had to have his way in life. The only thing she needed to use was caution to guard her heart or this billionaire would break it far more than Edward had. Now, when she looked back at her engagement, she wondered if she had been in love with Edward at all.

She unbuckled and scooted close to Chase, to rest her hand on his thigh. Speeding along the private road, he put his arm around her.

"You're living dangerously, unbuckling now."

"I trust you totally to take care of us," she said, laughing. "Besides, we have the road to ourselves."

He gave her a quick searching glance. "This is damn good, Laurel. I knew it would be," he said.

The winding road followed the ocean, and she watched waves break over boulders that thrust up and out of the water. Windswept cypress branches stretched skyward.

"This is a spectacular place and an awesome view," she said.

"I think so. I'm glad you're getting to see it for your arrival because at the moment it's a clear day. Later, the fog may come in and hide our surroundings. Either way, it's peaceful here and I can relax." Ahead she saw tall wrought-iron gates, which swung wide on Chase's approach. "I have a privacy fence except on the ocean side, and none of the help will be at the house, but they live nearby. I have some people who handle security and they're around. You just won't see them."

"You seem totally isolated here."

"That's what I like. I don't bring people here with me." He glanced at her. "You're a first."

"I'm flattered but curious," she said, stroking his thigh lightly. He inhaled and rubbed her arm where his hand rested. "Why did you bring me here?"

"I knew you wouldn't go far away, and I want to be alone with you where we won't be disturbed by business or family or anything else," he said, glancing at her. "I have plans for us for the weekend," he added in a thick voice that caused her heart to beat faster.

"Your family has been here, haven't they? Your cousins?"

"No. You really are the first."

Startled, she stared at him. "I'm learning all sorts of things about you. You must like being alone, don't you?"

"Yes. A lot of the time," he answered. "I've

told you that I had a house filled with brothers and sisters growing up—six of us, four boys and two girls and I'm the oldest. Thankfully, I had hiding places on the ranch where I could get off to myself." She studied his profile, his thick eyelashes and prominent cheekbones.

"Amazing you're so social and yet so solitary. You can be quite charming, even though I shouldn't tell you, because you already know it too well."

He laughed. "I'm happy to discover that you think I can be charming."

"You know women find you captivating. You even won over my grandmother. That takes a bit of doing, particularly when she's not happy with us about this weekend."

"She's a shrewd woman, and frankly I'm glad I don't have to see her often. It's been a long time since someone made me feel as if I were sixteen again and needed to watch my manners."

Laurel laughed softly. "That's Gramma. She has that effect on people, but she has kept us all in line much more than my dad. Or mom, too, for that matter."

"I'm surprised your dad was so into enjoying life if she keeps a tight rein on the family."

"I think he charmed her, just as you did."

"What about your mom? Was she a stern force?"

"Sometimes with us, but never with my dad. She was so in love with Dad and charmed by him that he could do no wrong in her eyes," Laurel said, gazing outside but seeing her parents. "I hope I'm never that much in love with any man!" she exclaimed.

"That's a little scary for any man to hear," Chase remarked, bringing her back to the moment.

"You needn't worry. It will never apply to you and me."

"I don't want to marry and you don't want to be wildly in love with someone. Seems to sum up our feelings about relationships. I'm surprised."

"I want to remain my own person and be able to see the other person as human, not invincible. Mom thought Dad could do no wrong. That wasn't the case."

"You sound as if you don't approve of his lifestyle."

She shrugged. "My dad could be frivolous and maybe flighty. There were times Mom should have said no."

"That kind of love is admirable, though. My folks are in love, I suppose. I've never thought much about it. They stay together and they seem compatible, but each has created his own life and they don't spend time together except for a couple of hours at the end of the day."

She glanced at him. "I haven't told anyone this, Chase. Even Gramma doesn't know. After Dad went into the hospital, he told me that he got deeply into gambling debts."

"Oh, damn," Chase remarked under his breath. "That's why you were selling everything," he said and she nodded.

"Yes. Dad took out loans to pay off the debts. He's longtime friends with Mitch Anson, so Mitch approved the loans. For years Mom used to go with him to Vegas, so I knew he gambled. He told me he never played for high stakes while Mom was alive. After she died a few years ago, he piled up big debts. He mortgaged the ranch and took out loans against it and the hotel. Thank heavens he paid off the gambling debts with the loans and I don't have to deal with those people. I accepted your offer to pay off his loans."

"You've been able to, haven't you?"

"Easily, now, thanks to you," she remarked dryly. "That's all confidential, but that's part of why I couldn't say no to you."

"You've made a lot of sacrifices for your family. That's commendable," he said and she shrugged.

"I love them and they love me, and I have some responsibilities for them." Laurel turned to look out the window as a sprawling, clapboard house came into view. Outbuildings were farther in the distance, almost hidden by tall cypress. "This is a spellbinding place," she said, "with the ocean and the cypress."

"I've always liked it," he said. They parked in back and in minutes she stepped into a large living area with a vaulted ceiling that ran above the second floor. Light poured through skylights high above them as well as through two-story-high panes of glass along one wall. Extending from the kitchen was an area that held a breakfast table and hutch. Adjoining the informal dining area and kitchen was a sitting area that held maroon leather sofas and chairs and where a massive stone fireplace filled one corner.

"This is spectacular, Chase," she said, looking around. "The view is awesome!" She gazed at the ocean and its whitecaps as the waves rolled in.

"Thanks," he replied. "Come upstairs and I'll show you where we'll be."

He tossed his hat on a chair as they entered an expansive hallway that had a wide, curving staircase. She followed him into a sitting room bathed in light through floor-to-ceiling glass windows. One wall held a large stone fireplace, and two area rugs were on the maple floors. Through an open door she could see the adjoining bedroom with a king-size bed. "This is a wonderful place," she said, gazing through the tall windows and getting an even better look at the ocean. The house sat on one side of curved land, and she could see the waves washing against the rocks and cliff on the other side of the curve.

"Laurel," Chase said, his tone entirely different. "Come here. I have something for you."

He held out a box wrapped in blue tissue and tied with a blue satin ribbon.

Though she knew it wasn't an engagement ring, her heart still soared at the prospect.

She was in deeper trouble than she thought.

Eight

Her heart thudding, Laurel opened the box to find a huge diamond pendant surrounded by smaller diamonds. "Chase, it's fabulous!" she exclaimed, amazed he would give her such a gift.

Chase stepped around her and fastened it behind her neck. "You're what's fantastic. I want you to remember today."

She turned and modeled it for him, then wound her arms around his neck. "Thank you! It's dazzling and how could I ever forget this day? And I intend to see to it that you don't forget it either," she whispered.

His gaze consumed her. "I've waited for what seems like an eternity. I want you more than you can ever know," he said.

He leaned forward to kiss her, drawing her more tightly into his embrace, and his expression grew solemn.

He kissed her until she forgot the gift and could think only about Chase.

His sizzling kisses sent her temperature soaring. Desire heightened and she moaned softly. Her breasts became sensitive and tingled. For now she would seize what she could from these moments with him because there was a fabulous hot chemistry between them.

This weekend, as well as the entire month, she could remove both physical and emotional barriers. Eagerly, she wanted to explore his marvelous body, to discover every inch of him. She intended to see to it that he didn't walk away easily at the end of the month, and she wanted to feel that he would never forget her.

"Laurel, my love," he whispered, and she knew the endearment meant nothing to him, that he merely mouthed it in the throes of passion.

"Love me," she whispered, wanting his hands and mouth and body on her. His tongue stroked hers and his hands roamed over her. She didn't notice as he twisted buttons free, but her blouse fell to the floor, followed by her red slacks. She kicked away her shoes and impatiently tugged off his shirt and unfastened his trousers to let them drop. Keys jingled and his belt buckle clinked. She paused to frame his face with her hands.

"I hope you never forget this afternoon," she whispered, and his eyes changed to the color of a stormy sea. He held her away to let his gaze run over her.

"I want to kiss every inch of you. You take my breath away, and I want to look at you end-lessly—I want to touch and caress and kiss you. I intend to see what excites you and make you lose all that cool control," he said.

His words were an aphrodisiac. She simmered beneath his gaze, eagerly reaching for him. Gasping with pleasure as she arched her hips against him, she felt his thick arousal. She hooked her fingers in his briefs and freed him from them.

All reason and resolutions were demolished, and she relished his loving. Showering kisses on her throat, he unclasped her bra. It fell on her feet, but she gave no heed.

He cupped her breasts in his large, tanned hands, and his thumbs lazed back and forth across her taut peaks, making her gasp. She grabbed his strong forearms, inhaling and surrendering to the intense pleasure streaking from his touch.

"You're perfection," he whispered in a rasp. "You don't have any idea what you do to me," he said, leaning closer to circle her nipple with his tongue. Hot and wet, each stroke increased her need for him. Deep and low inside her, heat burned, heightening desire. He was male perfection and she drank in the sight of him. She kissed him hungrily and then scattered her kisses down, kneeling to circle his thick manhood with her hand. As he wound his fingers in her hair, he inhaled deeply.

With a pounding heartbeat, she ran her hands along his strong legs slowly. At the same time the tip of her tongue traced circles on his belly and his fingers clenched handfuls of her hair. Pleasure grew as she stroked his thick rod and then took him into her mouth, running her tongue over him.

With a gasp he pulled her to her feet, wrapping one arm around her and leaning over her to kiss her hard. Their mouths fused, he swept her up into his arms and carried her to bed, flinging back covers and placing her on the bed. She was on fire with need, her body clamoring for him.

He moved to her foot and ran his tongue upward along the inside of her shapely leg, and she writhed with pleasure, her fists knotting the bedding. She opened her legs to him and his hand dallied over her intimately, rubbing and caressing her.

"Chase," she whispered, watching him as he knelt between her legs. He was thick and ready. She couldn't get enough of looking at his superb body. She memorized the sight of him. His broad shoulders and chest always stirred her desire.

He caressed the inside of her thigh, his fingers drifting lightly to her soft folds.

Closing her eyes, she arched beneath his touch, raising her hips for more, wanting him inside her with an urgency that was becoming unbearable.

Soon he lay beside her, tangling his legs with hers as his fingers continued touching her intimately, rubbing her and driving her wild, making her thrash beneath his touch. "Chase!" she cried out and he kissed her, silencing her.

With a cry she broke away and pushed him down. "Let me love you," she said, turning him over and moving astride him, starting at the backs of his knees to trace wet kisses up the backs of his legs, stroking his firm bottom and then sliding up to caress his smooth, muscled back until she reached his nape. He turned, wrapping an arm around her while he kissed her and his other hand explored her as thoroughly as she had him.

Still kissing her, he rolled over, taking her with him, and then he climbed off the bed, pulling open a drawer in a bedside table to get a condom.

"I'm on the pill," she said, clasping his wrist to stop him.

While he moved back between her legs, she drank in the sight of him, running the tips of her fingers over his strong legs, caressing his manhood. Kissing her, he lowered himself, and she wrapped her arms around him and closed her eyes.

She slid her hands down to cup his bottom and pull him toward her. "Love me, Chase," she whispered until he kissed her again and her words were lost.

Thick and hard, he eased into her and she gasped, wrapping her long legs around him and arching beneath him as he withdrew.

"Chase!" she cried. "I want you!"

He eased in again, slowly filling her, and she arched again to meet him, writhing with longing for his loving.

He was covered with a sheen of sweat. She stroked his back, wishing she could drive him to lose his iron control the way she'd lost hers. She moved wildly, clinging to him as her head thrashed and she moaned with pleasure and need. "Love me!" she gasped.

Still he held off, tension steadily building. And then his control disintegrated and he pumped furiously, filling her, hot and hard. Lights exploded behind her closed eyelids. Her thundering pulse drowned all sounds as together they moved frantically until she felt him shudder with release.

"Laurel! My love!" he exclaimed.

She cried out when the release burst inside her in a dazzling climax enveloping her in rapture.

While she tried to catch her breath, she floated back to reality. She could feel his heart pounding as violently as her own.

Relishing touching him, she ran her hands over him feeling a closeness and union that wiped out all constraints and differences. He was marvelous, breathtaking, handsome. At this moment he was united with her and she basked in satisfaction and satiation.

Turning, he showered her temple with light

kisses, trailing them to her ear. "You're fabulous," he whispered, his breath hot.

"I can say the same about you," she purred, opening her eyes to find him watching her intently. The moment was aglow and his expression held joy and satisfaction.

"You're more than I dreamed of and hoped for," he whispered, trailing kisses on her cheek to her mouth to kiss her lightly. He raised his head again to look at her. "So much more," he whispered. "I feel like I was empty until you came along."

She trembled, his words the first intrusion of reality and the world they'd temporarily left behind. She wanted to believe the fabulous things he was saying, but he was a charmer and she knew better, and now she wished he had kept silent and held the moment between them with its euphoria.

"The loving is fantastic," she said softly, knowing that she was being truthful with him. She wouldn't mouth endearments she didn't mean, empty lies that he might believe although he should know better, since he did such things himself.

He rolled over, taking her with him and turning on his side, still holding her close. "I could hold you for the entire night. I don't want you out of my arms."

"I would like it if you did," she answered, winding her fingers in his chest hair, feeling the short, crisp hair tickle her breasts.

"You said you're opposed to marriage because of your parents. Is that really the whole reason, Chase?" she blurted out, surprising herself.

His jaw firmed and he gazed beyond her. "It's more than enough reason. I've watched my dad spend his whole life working like crazy for his family. He married young and started a family, so Dad has been bogged down with responsibility his entire life. He's tied to the ranch. He's never traveled, never partied, never developed hobbies because he took care of the ranch and his family."

A sharp pain twisted her insides while her anger flared. She thought of Edward and how he'd broken their engagement the moment she'd taken responsibility for her family. Chase was the same, wanting to avoid anything that interfered with his life and what he wanted to do. She knew she had to let go of her anger for now, forget that Chase was so focused on himself. She tried to turn her attention back to what he was saying to her.

"Mom and Dad have never done anything except work. Only Dad is worse than my mom. She at least gets out and meets her sisters and goes back to Texas to her family. Dad and my Montana grandparents have spent lifetimes working and being tied down. They've never traveled, never had a social life, nothing. All the years I was growing up, I saw marriage as a trap. I still get claustrophobic when I contemplate it, and I've never, ever been in love." He looked down at her.

"You got it with both barrels," he added softly, his voice changing as he smiled at her. "You touched a nerve, as you can see. Most women don't believe me and don' t ask or they feel the way I do and view marriage as a trap or they've been married and it went sour and they don't ever want to do that again."

"You sound bitter," she said, aghast at his view of marriage. He was no more a man to love than Edward had been, in spite of how wonderful a time she had when she was with Chase. She touched his jaw. "My parents were happy, and no one could ever describe my dad as being 'tied down.' He didn't travel a lot, but they went places, with and without us, and my dad loves people and parties. He made the most of being married, and I think he loved Mom deeply and she loved him."

"That wasn't the view of marriage I ever had, and you couldn't possibly have been describing my parents. It makes my blood run cold to consider being trapped for the rest of my life the way my dad is," Chase said, nuzzling her throat and then kissing her lightly.

"Perhaps he doesn't feel trapped. Maybe he would have lived that way had he been single all his life," she said, and Chase's eyebrows arched.

"I guess he would have, but it's hard to imagine. I'll never know, but I know what I don't want."

"You don't find it better to be with someone, more exciting, more entertaining? Reassuring when life takes a bad turn? But then, your life must not take bad turns."

"Of course it does, at least occasionally. And yes, it's definitely better to be with you right now than off by myself. I would never have the excitement I do now if I weren't with you." He leaned away and let his hand slide down over her breasts, and she pressed her hips against him as a tremor of desire rocked her.

His eyes darkened and he kissed her, brushing her lips first and then kissing her more passionately. She could feel him stir.

"Chase!" she whispered, running her hand along his hip, feeling the short hairs on his thigh. "You're supposed to be exhausted and quiet and not aroused."

"Parts of me don't know that, and all of me is responding to you," he answered as he kissed her throat and caressed her breasts.

"I should shower."

"We can do better than that. Don't move," he said, extricating himself and crossing the bedroom. She watched him, relishing looking at his strong body, feeling a pang over the circumstances she was thrown into with Chase.

In minutes he returned and picked her up. She wrapped her arms around his neck and smiled at him, and he paused as he looked into her eyes and smiled in return.

"We're going to shower?"

"I told you, better than that," he said, carrying her into a large bathroom with a huge marble Jacuzzi tub, partially filled with water. He walked down steps into the tub and sat, holding her on his lap.

She could feel his arousal pressed against her and her desire rekindled. She twisted around and the minute she looked into his eyes, she saw the desire she felt, mirrored there.

She wound her arm around his neck and pulled his head down to kiss him, her heartbeat speeding. He lifted her easily so she sat astride him and then he thrust into her and she moved on him. He fondled her breasts, cupping them as his tongue circled her nipple, first one and then the other until he groaned and held her, moving his hips against her.

Wildly she thrashed on him until she climaxed again as he did. Draping herself over him, she gasped for breath while pleasure filled her. She felt boneless, warm and satisfied, pressing against him until she climbed off to sit between his long legs and lean back against him. He held her and nuzzled her neck, kissing her ear.

"Best bath ever," he whispered.

"I'd agree with that," she replied, running her hand along his legs. "You're a fantastic lover."

"Thanks," he said. "I'm glad you think so. This is good, Laurel. Damn good. It's better than I thought it would be, because you're fantastic."

"Thank you, kind sir. Pure flattery but delightful to hear," she said, feeling giddy and realizing that she was going to fall head over heels in love with this man and there was no way to stop it from happening unless she walked out on him today. And *that* was impossible. She would have to back out of their deal to do that. He was too likable. She thought of the reasons she should avoid falling in love, first and foremost, knowing that he would never return her feelings.

"This is the way a bath should be," he said, his hands caressing her breasts.

She inhaled and captured his hands, holding them in hers. "What will you do with my hotel, Chase?"

"Use if for my people who won't be living in Montana on a more permanent basis. It'll be there for employees who will come and go. Probably let Brice continue to run it, since he's done that for years and is competent and recommended by you."

"He's excellent, but he told me this morning that he's taken a job with the Barclay Champion Hotel and he'll leave when I no longer need him and I turn things over to you and your staff."

"Although I'm not surprised, I'm sorry to hear

that, because I'd just as soon keep competent people and the transition smooth."

"He's a great manager. Our employees have been with us a long time. They hire on and stay."

"That's a tribute to your dad, then."

"Dad and Brice. My dad didn't ever stay at work 24/7 the way you've said yours does, and Brice takes over when he's gone. Without Dad there, we need someone who is totally reliable. Anyway, I hope you do forgive Brice."

"I'm thankful we weren't in the front lobby and on the evening news."

"I hadn't even thought of that," she said. "How awful that would have been! I would have never heard the end of it about this weekend."

"Well, it wasn't, so we don't have to worry. When we get back, Laurel, will you move into my suite with me?"

"That's the deal we made," she remarked dryly.

"I hope the time comes when you can stop focusing on the deal we made and you don't sound so bitter about it. Even more, I'm looking forward to reaching a time when you don't have any anger toward me," he whispered, his breath warm on the back of her neck as he toyed with locks of her hair.

Her anger had vanished from the time they

walked into his house. It might return, but she doubted if she would ever be as annoyed as before. She would have to deal with hurt later because after one month of his loving and charm, she couldn't guess how long it would take her to get over him.

How many broken hearts did he have in his past? She suspected a large number, and she hadn't intended for that to happen to her.

"So, do we get to eat around here?" she asked, putting her head back against his shoulder.

"If I can stop loving you long enough to get food on the table."

"Maybe I should get our dinner on the table," she said.

"Let me see if I can get your mind off food," Chase said in a husky voice and then lifted her around to kiss her.

It was past midnight before they were wrapped in robes, seated on a sofa in the sitting room in front of a roaring fire Chase had built. He raised his glass of wine. "Here's to the best night of my life," he said quietly.

Smiling, she shook her head. "That's absurd, Chase! Probably the best night was the time you made your first million. Why do I suspect you've made the same toast other nights in the past?"

"This is the best night," he replied solemnly. "Making money is always fine, but it can't give me the high you have in the past few hours."

Unable to believe him, she looked down and swirled her wine. "This is better than I expected, I will admit that." She glanced around. "I can see why you like the solitude and to come up here alone, yet at night this must be a lonely place."

"I love it here. Since this is the first time I've brought anyone, I'm glad it's you, and I'm happy you accepted my offer and that we came here."

She realized she wouldn't be back, but everything with Chase was temporary.

"You've sold the hotel and taken your ranch off the market. Have you decided what you'll do now?" he asked. "Go back to Dallas for a time? Go back and forth? You have more choices."

She nodded. "I'll stay around here because of Dad, although I'll go back sometime soon for a couple of days. I'll stay in touch better than just by fax and e-mail and phone, as I've been doing."

"I'll fly to Dallas with you soon, and we'll look at lawns you've done. Maybe I can hire you."

"I'm expensive."

"I'm rich," he said, smiling at her as she laughed.

"Very well. I have a portfolio if you want to see."

"Sure," he replied, sipping his wine. "I can't wait to look at your portfolio and whatever else you'll show me," he said in a suggestive tone.

"Strictly business, Chase. I didn't mean here—I don't carry it with me," she said. "When we get back, you can come to my office and I'll show you."

"For this next week I want to clear my calendar. I'd like to stay here with you. Can you do that?"

"The whole week here?" she asked in surprise. Eagerness flared over the prospect of spending that much uninterrupted time with him. She thought about the responsibilities in Montana and Texas. "I suppose I can because anyone who needs to get in touch with me will be able to," she said.

"Excellent," Chase exclaimed, placing her wineglass on a table beside his. He moved closer and pulled her on his lap and wrapped his arms around her. "I want you here where we can make love day and night."

Her heart skipped a beat, and she ran her fingers through his hair. "I'll second that suggestion," she said and he grinned. She had tossed aside reluctance, worries and resentment for now, suspending caution and enjoying Chase, determined that she would see to it that he wouldn't forget her easily and allow her to fade and blend into his memories of other women who had briefly passed through his life.

He pulled loose the tie to her robe and shoved it off her shoulders, cupping her breasts in his hands. "You're gorgeous," he whispered and leaned closer to circle her taut peak with his tongue.

Gasping with pleasure, she tangled her fingers in his hair, tossing her head back and letting him love her until the torment became too intense.

Hours later, after a snack, as she was once more in his arms in bed, she caressed his bare shoulder. "You are an insatiable animal," she whispered, and he chuckled softly as he traced the shape of her ear with his finger.

"I think I can say the same. You're a tempestuous woman, even more passionate than I expected, and you respond to the slightest touch, which sets me on fire."

"I hope so," she purred with satisfaction. "I

want to drive you to lose your strong control and torment you as you do me."

"Sounds good to me. We'll work on that tonight," he said, sitting up. He stood and picked her up to carry her to his shower, where he set her on her feet. As he turned on warm water, she ran her hands over his marvelous body, and in minutes showering was forgotten.

Light, gray and dim, spilled into the room. Laurel lay against Chase in the crook of his arm with her leg thrown over his. "Are you ever going to feed me a real meal, or am I simply a sex object?"

"You are definitely a sex object," he replied with amusement, toying with locks of her soft hair. "A wanton, torrid, red-hot lover. How can I think about food if you're around?"

"You better think about it before I starve and waste away and can't make love to you. The last time you told me we'd eat, I had about three sips of wine and that was it."

"Waste away, huh?" he teased, running his hand over her hip and then cupping her breast while his thumb circled her nipple and she inhaled. "I don't think you're exactly going to disappear. You feel solid, soft, warm—definitely enough of you there to set me on fire again."

"Will you stop," she said, laughing and catching his hand as she lay back against his shoulder. He rolled on his side to look down at her.

"I can't stop making love to you, but I'll try to get something for you to eat. You better cover up from your chin to your toes, though, if you want me to leave you alone while you cook breakfast. Or if you prefer, since you missed dinner, I'll cook a huge breakfast."

"I will do exactly that. Even better," she said, wriggling away from him and sliding across the bed to get out on the far side. "I will shower *alone* and you can go cook. I got in a rush yesterday to get ready to go and missed lunch."

"I wish I thought you'd done that because you were so eager to begin this weekend," he said, and for once she didn't hear the teasing note in his voice. Startling her, she looked at him and saw he was watching her with a sober expression.

"I was eager, Chase," she answered in a tone as solemn as his, and he slid off the bed to step toward her. She held up her hand.

"Just wait—"

"After you say something like that to me, I can't keep from reaching for you."

"You're not coaxing me back to bed until I've had food."

"Now that is a challenge," he said, approaching her, but now his eyes were twinkling, so she scooped up her robe to yank it on and turned and ran. Behind her, she heard his chuckle. She knew if he really wanted to catch her, he easily could. When he wanted, he could move like lightning, but he let her go. She rushed to shower and get into some clothes, wondering if she would even be able to keep them on through the meal or get more than a couple of bites down before they made love again. And for a minute there he'd sounded as if he'd meant what he'd said.

In the shower she was wrapped in euphoria, daydreaming of Chase's marvelous body, his strong muscles and his untiring energy. He was a marvel in bed and she tingled, thinking about their lovemaking. She also blushed while remembering moments with him.

She gave vent to erotic images until she was hot and wanting him again as if they hadn't made love again and again since the first moment they walked into his house.

She dressed in a black bra that was a wisp of lace and a matching black thong. She pulled on red silk lounging pajamas, the top tight and very low cut. She'd never worn the pajamas before, but for now, shut away alone with Chase, it suited her.

She found him outside on a lighted redwood deck, a fire burning in a large cast-iron chiminea as he stood grilling sausage and ham. Food smelled enticing but not half as tempting as Chase. With her pulse speeding, she looked at him in his tight jeans, black knit shirt and loafers. She walked up quietly behind him and wrapped her arms around him, her hands on his chest.

"You handsome devil," she said in a throaty voice. Turning, he wrapped her in his embrace, leaning down to kiss her thoroughly until she pushed against his chest.

"Chase, don't burn up breakfast."

"Why not? I'm already on fire," he said quietly and then noticed her clothes, holding her away slightly to take a more thorough look. "You look red-hot and I'd like to take you right back to bed."

"Don't you dare! Feed me first or I'll get really surly."

"Surly? I don't believe it," he said. He pulled

her up against his chest. "I'll feed you and then I'll seduce you."

"Sounds like a deal to me," she drawled in a breathy voice, and she ran her hand lightly over his manhood, which was already aroused. He inhaled and his eyes darkened.

"Laurel," he cautioned. "You keep that up and breakfast is postponed."

"I think you'll keep it up," she said softly, twisting out of his arms and walking away.

She heard the fork he'd been holding clatter on the cooker, and as she started to look over her shoulder, he caught up with her and pulled her into his embrace to kiss her fervently again until she pushed against him.

"You go cook and I'll leave you alone," she said breathlessly. "Can I get anything on the table?"

He took a deep breath and shook his head, turning away without a word and she knew he'd lost all interest in food. Smiling to herself, she walked away. She'd rather be in his arms and wanted to make love, but she hoped to make him want her to a degree he had never felt before. Also, she was almost faint with hunger.

Finally, breakfast was served. They devoured

only about half when he stood, and picked her up and carried her to the bedroom where the next hours were spent in lovemaking.

By Monday morning, after they'd showered together, she lay in bed in Chase's arms again. She wound her fingers in the thick mat of curls across his chest as she listened to his deep breathing. "Chase, we've spent all our time since arriving either in bed or making love, with just a few minutes between to shower or eat. That is truly decadent."

"Is this a complaint?" he asked, his voice laced with amusement.

She rose up to look at him, tracing the line of his jaw that had a night's growth of dark stubble. "Definitely not a complaint, only amazement."

He grinned. "It's been damn great." He twirled a long lock of her hair around his finger. "I can't think of one better way to spend my time," he added, his voice becoming solemn as his gaze traveled over her features and then lingered on her mouth.

"I know that look. I do want to eat breakfast because there's no telling when I'll get to eat again."

"You seem to require regular feeding."

"More or less," she stated dryly.

He propped his head on his hand to look at her. "You're beautiful. I want you more each day, instead of less," he said, once again a rare moment when he sounded earnest and convincing, yet she knew she shouldn't give much heed to such words.

That was the way she felt about him and his marvelous body, but she wasn't going to tell him. "Today, I need some time to call the hotel and check on things and talk to Gramma and see about my dad."

"Sure," he said, leaning the last few inches to kiss her senseless.

It was almost noon before she got away to the study, where she closed the door and called the hotel to talk to Brice, writing a list of things he told her and listening to problems—*a lot* of problems.

Then, lost in thought about the weekend, she stared at her reflection in a mirror without really seeing herself. She had dressed in jeans and a blue shirt, with her hair in a ponytail, and it amazed her to realize it was the first time she'd put on her regular clothes since her arrival Saturday. "Is your heart still intact?" she whispered to her image. "Are you falling in love with him?"

She thought she could honestly say no and walk away when the month was over, yet at the same time she had to admit she was having a wonderful time with him. "I hope not," she whispered, feeling hollow inside at the thought of parting from him.

When the month ends, I will be gone. She could remember him saying that to her, and she shivered. No matter what she did, he wasn't going to fall in love.

She looked at the notes she'd made and left the study to find Chase, to tell him about Athens' news. It wasn't good. He sat in his office with papers spread in front of him.

"Ready for an interruption?" she asked and he motioned for her to come in. Through the window behind him, she could see that fog had rolled in and it was difficult to see far, yet she could make out the breakers crashing against rocks. "I need to talk to you," she said, wondering if their euphoria was about to come to an end.

Nine

Laurel sat across from Chase, and her breath sped as she looked at his broad shoulders in a knit shirt that still revealed his muscles. As her gaze traveled over him, she thought about him naked, holding her. Desire stirred and momentarily she forgot why she had come to see him.

"Yes?" he asked, his eyebrows arching with curiosity, bringing her back to the moment. Her cheeks flushed over her erotic daydreams.

"I was thinking about something else," she said, rattling a paper in her hand.

"It must have been interesting," he said, one corner of his mouth curling in amusement.

"Chase, I called the hotel to check on things, and Ty has called twice, so I returned his call."

"And I assume he's unhappy with me. Or more accurately, with my people."

"That's right. They are really pressuring Ty to sell and buying out land around him and threatening him to make it more difficult for him if he doesn't cooperate. Those are horrible tactics." As she talked, his expression remained the same except a coldness filled his eyes.

"Look, Laurel, I don't tell you how to run your business. I need that land. You said yourself that you could see why it would be more convenient for me to own the Carson ranch."

"Chase, for a brief time can you stop viewing the world from the standpoint of what you want? Think about the Carsons and their family place. You're not a sentimental man, obviously, so it's a stretch, but for once put aside your own selfish wants and take a good look at the situation to see if you can find another solution," she said heatedly. She knew she was losing her temper with him, which wasn't going to help matters and could make things worse. She suspected people close to Chase seldom corrected him or told him what he should do. "Do it another way besides owning his property."

He clamped his jaw closed and glared at her and she glared back.

"Is this going to make a difference between us?" he asked quietly.

"Not really. My emotions aren't all tied up in my relationship with you anyway, and yours aren't with me," she snapped.

His eyebrows arched. "You run roughshod over my feelings, and as I've told you before, I don't usually bomb out to this extent with a woman. Particularly not after spending time with her."

"You're charming and handsome and ever so appealing," she said. "You're not bombing out, but I'm not so gaga that I can't think straight."

She thought she saw the corner of his mouth twitch, but she wasn't certain. While she couldn't tell what his reaction really was, she suspected he was less than happy with her. Silence stretched in the room, and tension wound tighter as she stared back at him and wondered what was running through his mind.

Finally he picked up the phone and made a call, leaning back in his chair.

She listened as he talked to Luke Perkins.

"Luke, stop dealing with Ty Carson. Make an appointment for me to see him a week from today. I'll talk to him. I'll see if we can lease some land from him and pay him to get water from his place. That way his damn ranch will stay intact and still be his." Chase swiveled his chair around and spoke softly and she couldn't hear the conversation. She suspected Luke wasn't happy with Chase's decision, but she was thrilled that he had backed off buying Ty's ranch.

Knowing that he had done this solely for her, she stood impatiently, bubbling and happy.

"That's right," Chase said emphatically into the phone. "Thanks."

As he broke the connection and turned to replace the receiver of his phone, she rushed to sit in his lap and hug him. "Thank you!" She kissed him hard.

Quickly, his arm circled her waist and he kissed her in return. His fingers went to the buttons of her shirt to unfasten them, and she tugged his shirt out of his jeans and pulled it over his head. In minutes he carried her to the sofa to peel off her jeans and shed his.

It was an hour later after lovemaking that she lay in his arms on the wide sofa and remembered the phone call. "Chase, thank you for planning to go see Ty and deciding to ask him if you can lease part of his ranch. Thank you so much!"

He smiled at her. "You're too softhearted, darlin'."

"I know you're doing that for me. Don't make me fall in love with you."

His smile broadened. "That would be bad? I'm head over heels in love."

"No, you're not," she replied, combing locks of hair off his forehead and running her fingers down to his jaw. "You're head over heels in lust, and there is a monumental difference."

"Back to the marriage theme," he said in a resigned voice. "I can be in love."

"You told me that you never had been in love in your life."

"Not the kind that leads to marriage, like you're talking about," he answered dryly.

"There, see. You're not in the kind of love now that leads to long-term commitment or marriage. Therefore, you do mean lust."

"Call it want you will—to me, I'm in love and I want you."

"Yet not permanently," she repeated in exasperation. "The more we talk, the more I realize I can stop worrying about falling in love with you."

"In that case," he said, rolling over and picking her up, "we'll go shower and stop this discussion. I want you grateful, wanting to please me and thank me and in love with me."

"You want it all, don't you?" she asked him, smiling at him, yet knowing he was definitely deep in lust and nothing more. But she was grateful to Chase concerning the Carson ranch, and it made her feel better toward him to find that he wasn't as hard-hearted and cold as she had thought.

Early on Sunday morning, Chase stirred first and looked at Laurel, sleeping against him. He turned carefully on his side to see her better. Her blond hair was spread across the pillow. This past week with her had been fabulous, so much more than he'd expected and he didn't want to go back to work tomorrow and give up having her to himself.

He had no illusions; she wasn't in love with him. Far from it. He couldn't think of any woman he'd ever spent time with and given so much attention to who had been as cool as Laurel. He suspected that if their deal was declared off today, she'd be packed and gone, which he had to admit bothered him. Women he was interested in were usually in love with him and he had always been the one to walk on the relationship. He knew he wouldn't be the one in this case. It would be Laurel.

She stayed because she was keeping her part of a bargain with him, yet there was a hot chemistry between them that had grown hotter with each passing day. That was what amazed him.

He'd expected to spend a weekend away with her, enjoy his month with her and walk away forgetting her totally, as he had from affairs in the past. He still thought he'd feel that way at the end of the month, but he didn't want to think about leaving California today. In spite of work piling up in Montana and Texas, he wondered whether he could talk her into staying longer because when they returned to Athens, there would be demands on his time as well as hers and they'd never get the opportunity, intimacy and privacy they'd had here.

He pushed down the sheet, letting his gaze drink in the sight of her nude. He was already aroused and wanted to wake her and love her, but he also liked looking at her. He traced a circle on her breast, and she stirred in a slow, sensuous move. He leaned down to trace around her nipple with his tongue and then raised his head to look into her eyes, which were sleepy yet filled with desire.

He ached to possess her. Wrapping her arms around his neck, she pulled him down to kiss him. As he embraced her and moved above her, he kissed her and desire escalated.

Tangling one hand in her hair, he stroked her silky skin. She was all softness and curves, bewitching and seductive.

She pushed him over and straddled him, shifting to lavish kisses over him. He watched her while his temperature climbed and need built until he could no longer wait and moved over her to spread her legs and enter her. Wanting to make it last and draw out ecstasy, he thrust slowly.

"Darlin', you're awesome," he whispered.

"Come here, Chase," she said, pulling his head down to kiss him, and words were gone as he filled her and withdrew to fill her again, soon pumping until he climaxed with her, crashing over an edge and sinking down to hold her tightly.

As they lay on their sides with their legs entangled, he stroked her damp hair from her face.

"Laurel, this is good between us, really good.

Let's stay two or three days more. I can move my work around, and you've sold the hotel, so you don't have the responsibilities you did."

She frowned at him, and as he waited for her to answer, he realized he badly wanted her to accept. At the hotel she'd move in with him anyway. He thought about his calendar, which was packed with appointments for the coming week, but Luke could juggle them around, postpone them or attend in his place in some cases.

"This is something special, darlin'," Chase admitted, surprised by the depth of need he had. He traced his hand along her throat.

Her blue eyes darkened and he saw desire stirring again, marveling at how easy it was to arouse her and how much she liked to make love.

"You know I might have to get back quickly."

"Same deal as when we first came—I can get you back on a moment's notice, and at the most we're only a little over two hours away. Let's stay two more days."

"When's the last time you took off more than a week?"

"Probably back in March," he said, knowing full well that it was less than a week and he planned for it months ahead of time. He took off a lot but not for long periods of time. Weekends, a few days during the week, usually were the most he'd do at a time.

"I've missed so much in Texas, Chase."

"You can miss a bit more," he said firmly, amazed at himself for pushing her and wanting her to say yes. He wondered how important she was becoming to him. Although every moment together he was becoming more emotionally entangled, he plunged ahead. "Stay and let's have the moment," he said.

"Very well," she said, sighing, and he had to laugh.

"There you go again, smashing what's left of my ego."

"No worries there," she add dryly, running her fingers along his bare shoulder. "I'll call home later and tell them when I'll return. So, how will you entertain me?" she asked, stretching with a teasing sparkle in her eyes and he laughed.

"How's this for a start?" he asked, leaning down to kiss her.

That evening as they sat eating grilled snapper fillets, Laurel sipped her wine and turned to look through the floor-to-ceiling windows. Fog rolled in over the ocean, and she knew it soon would envelope everything and visibility would be gone.

"I'd think it would be frightening and dangerous to be out there in a boat."

"Nowadays everyone has radar and sonar equipment and therefore they know where there are obstacles, but once upon a time it was probably damn frightening. I can show you some of the lighthouses along the coast, if you'd like."

"Yes, I would. Chase, I'll admit, I love this place."

"Me, too. This is my haven, more than the other homes I have." He stretched out his arm to caress her nape.

"I called the hotel. Brice was beside himself that I'm staying with you longer. I doubt if your people were happy either."

"I don't give a damn," Chase remarked. "Luke was shocked. I don't usually take this much time off at once," he said, raising his wine glass to her in a toast. "You're causing me to do things I've never done before. Here's to you, Laurel."

Thrilled by his statement, she raised her glass in return, toasting with him and wondering why he wanted to stay, because she'd be with him whether they were in Athens or California.

Brice had wanted her to return, and her grandmother's skepticism and disapproval were clearly discernible over the phone. She knew Ashley and Diana would think it was great because they had both been agog over Chase.

"This is a wonderful home," she said. "It's so quiet that you wouldn't know there's another person within a hundred miles."

"Actually, there are some people down the road and around the bend, but it seems that way and that's what I like."

They both sat quietly eating, but when they finished, Chase wanted her on his lap; soon she was wrapped in his embrace while they made love.

Tuesday afternoon, they packed and flew back to Montana. On the plane Chase took her hand. "I'll get someone to move your things to my suite. You can show them what to take."

"We're only across the hall," she remarked with amusement. "I'll bring my belongings when I need them. I can go back and forth."

"You can stay naked and I'll be happy."

"I'm sure you would be," she stated, laughing.

"Forget that one, Chase. We'll have so much work to catch up on."

"I want to go back to California next weekend. Will you go?"

"Perhaps, let me see if I get caught up, but I won't stay another week."

He nodded. "I'll need to see if I can get away, too."

She looked out the window of the plane. The first part of her month with him had passed so swiftly she was amazed. Not even three more full weeks and they would tell each other goodbye.

Reflecting on the past week, she studied Chase, acknowledging to herself that she had fallen in love with him. Love with such a charmer was never her intention, but it was impossible to prevent. She didn't want him to know it. She would have to get over it just as she had gotten over heartbreak with Edward. The nagging thought plaguing her was that she was in love with Chase, perhaps forever.

Wednesday morning Brice called and wanted to see her; Laurel could tell from the tone of his voice that he was unhappy.

Striding into her office and looking neat as usual in his brown suit, he raked his fingers through his hair. When he closed the door and sat facing her, his worried frown indicated the problem was large. "Laurel, I'll get to the point. Chase called me in this morning. He offered me triple my salary if I'd stay to work for him."

Joy for Brice was her first reaction. Once more Chase had been a good guy and had surprised her. Puzzled about Brice's scowl, she sat back in her chair. "I'd say that's wonderful news. He's not holding a grudge, and he recognizes the quality work you do. I'm glad he can afford to pay you more. I don't exactly see the problem."

"That's why I need to talk to you," Brice said, rubbing his hands together. She wondered what could be making him distraught when he'd had such a fantastic offer. "Soon your month with him will be over. If he breaks your heart, I couldn't bear to work for him."

Relief flooded her. "Brice, he won't break my heart. I promise," she said, feeling uneasy over making statements that weren't truthful. Each day she was growing more accustomed to having Chase in her life. Telling him goodbye would be a huge adjustment.

"You can't promise any such thing," Brice said as he studied her. "You're glowing right now, which means you've had a wonderful time with him. You stayed longer with him in California than you'd planned to. Whether or not you'll recognize it, Laurel, I think you're in love with him. I was there when you both came in last night, and anyone can see you're in love. You never looked like that with Edward. Frankly, he looks as if he's in love, too, but I doubt if the man can fall in love with anyone except himself."

She felt her face flush and bit back, telling Brice that he assumed too much. "I'm not going to fall in love. And even if I do, that has nothing to do with whether you accept his job offer or not."

"If he hurts you, I can't work for him. I'd hate him and feel responsible in a manner I never would have when your dad was here."

"Stop worrying. It's absolute foolishness," she stated, exasperated that people were worrying over her yet reminding herself they simply cared about her. "If you want to stay with the hotel, accept his fabulous offer and continue the wonderful job you do. Why go to a new place and start all over? Here you have the staff and conditions you like and your family seems happy. Have you and Deb talked it over?"

"Of course, and she wants me to accept and stay, but she understands my worry."

"Stop fretting needlessly." Smiling, she stood and walked around her desk to him. He came to his feet and she hugged him. "Accept the job. Grandmother, all of us, will feel better if you do. And don't worry about me. I'm not going to fall in love. He's still a wealthy playboy, and I haven't changed how I feel about that."

"You're not convincing me, but I may go ahead and accept."

"I'll be so happy if you do," she declared truthfully.

He clasped her lightly. "Thanks, Laurel. You take care of yourself. You just said it—Chase is another Edward."

"I know. I'll take care," she said and watched Brice leave.

She hurried down the hall to the office Chase had temporarily turned into his own. She walked through the outer office and knocked at his door.

Dressed in a tan suit, he looked up from his desk and came to his feet; her heartbeat quickened while business became secondary.

"I'll only be a minute because I have an appointment, but Brice came to see me," she said.

Chase closed his door, then put his arms around her waist.

"That was a fabulous offer you've given Brice, and I know he'll take it. That's wonderful—and once again, you're a good guy," she said, smiling.

"I wish you wouldn't always sound so damn surprised," he said solemnly. "I've missed you like hell."

"I'm not that far away," she reminded him. She reached up to kiss him, breaking away soon. She was breathless, filled with desire, and Chase was aroused.

"I have to go and you do, too. I'll see you tonight," she said.

Nodding, he inhaled deeply. As she left, her back tingled because she was certain he stood watching her.

Midafternoon, Chase called, saying he would be delayed and wouldn't be in until late that night.

With each hour her anticipation grew, and early in the evening she began to get ready for his arrival. She bathed and pulled on a new sheer black nightgown. Turning on soft music and building a fire, she was eager for him.

When he opened the door, she hurried to meet

him. Lights were low in his suite, and as she entered the front room, he dropped his coat on a chair and turned.

His gaze roamed over her, and in quick strides he reached her, pulling her to him. "Damn, you look good enough to eat," he whispered, and her answer was lost when he kissed her, picking her up to carry her to bed.

On the last Monday in August, Laurel met her grandmother at the hospital, and after an hour with Laurel's dad, they left for lunch together.

Halfway through lunch, her grandmother set down her glass of water. "How's Chase?"

"He's fine, Gramma. I've been with him to see the field his company is developing, and their plans sound impressive. The oil will make a difference in Montana's economy."

"That's all well and good, but it's you I want to know about. Are you happy?"

"Yes," Laurel answered honestly. "I am, except for worrying about Dad."

"We're all doing that. I don't want to see you hurt, and Chase doesn't seem like the type to marry."

"At this point in my life, I'm not ready for

marriage either, so that's okay," Laurel replied, feeling nervous about the turn in conversation.

"I hope. Edward hurt you and I can't help feeling that a second time with someone as charming as Chase—if you fall in love with him—will end with you hurt badly. Just be careful."

"Sometimes it's difficult to be careful where your heart is concerned," Laurel answered, smiling and reaching over to squeeze her grandmother's hand. "Thank you for worrying about me, though," she added.

"When your dad recovers, you'll go back to Dallas. What then with Chase?"

"I'll face that problem when it happens," she answered, knowing that she would have to tell Chase goodbye. Her grandmother continued to study her with a slight frown. "Gramma, don't worry. I'm fine."

"I pray you are, sweetie. He's far too likable."

She laughed, thinking her grandmother was right. "I'll tell him you said that. I think you scared him a little."

"Nonsense! That young man wouldn't be scared of the devil himself!" she said, and Laurel laughed again, knowing that would make Chase laugh, too.

When lunch was over, she kissed her grandmother goodbye and headed back to the hotel, deciding to start early getting ready for her dinner with Chase. She had only one more week with him and then they'd part. Forever.

On the desk in her office she kept a calendar that she watched carefully, aware of how swiftly August had ended and September had come. The closing came and went on September fourth. And suddenly it was the seventh of September, the night before their time together was over. She dressed with care in a long, backless, black silk dress with a plunging neckline. She left her hair down, and when he came through the door, she flew into his arms and dinner was promptly forgotten until long after midnight.

While he held her close against him in bed, Chase turned on his side to look at her. "Laurel, things have come up in my business, and I have to leave tomorrow and get back to Houston. I'm turning all the business here over to Luke, who can manage well without me."

Something twisted deep inside, but she was determined she wouldn't let him know.

He stroked her hair away from her face. "I want you to go with me. I can move your Dallas business, or you can keep it and I can open another one for you in Houston. I want you there. Will you go with me?" he asked, and her heart thudded because she wanted desperately to say yes.

Yet how could she?

Ten

Laurel looked at the handsome face that had become so important to her, his thick eyelashes and crystal-green eyes that darkened in passion, his sensual mouth, his prominent cheekbones and dark brown hair. Aching to accept, she stroked his cheek, knowing too well that later Chase would end their relationship and she would be hurt even more.

"Chase, it's been wonderful, but you said it all long ago—I'm geared for family. I don't want to go to Houston and be your mistress."

He inhaled and hugged her tightly. "I want you there. What we've had has been fantastic, Laurel," he said roughly and her pain deepened.

"You know that part of me wants to say yes," she answered truthfully, fighting tears, wanting to stay with him, "but the moment when we'd part would come, so I'll be hurt less if it's now," she stated with a knot in her throat.

"At least, give me another month," he said solemnly.

She slipped out of bed and pulled on her white silk robe. "I think we're finished, Chase. It's been fantastic, but it's over. I can't go to Houston with you. I have responsibility for my family. I've got a business in Dallas I can't go back to either because of my dad. I'm looking for a house in town to move my grandmother and the girls. They prefer that to moving to the hotel, and thanks to you and our month together, I can afford a house. When Dad recovers, he'll be there." She gazed into Chase's eyes, which were unreadable, and she had no idea how deeply he felt about what he had asked her.

"I need to stay here, and you have to go," she continued. "I won't be your mistress indefinitely, but this past month I've loved being with you," she added, unable to stop tears. She turned away and left, hurrying toward the door. Grabbing her purse, which still held the key to her suite, she rushed inside and closed the door, switching on a light. There hadn't been any footsteps behind her, and she realized that Chase had let her go and it really was over.

Blindly, she walked to a chair to sink down and put her head in her hands and cry, giving vent to her anguish. She had done exactly what she had promised herself she wouldn't do—fallen in love with him—and it hurt beyond any distress she had felt in parting with Edward. Chase had been the love of her life.

Even if she wanted to go with him to Houston, she wouldn't leave her family; yet questions tormented her. Would it be a way to hang on to him? If she went, would he eventually want to make the relationship permanent?

She knew she couldn't deal with his kind of temporary arrangement on a long-term basis, and she had responsibilities here.

She spent a sleepless, tearful night, finally falling into a restless sleep when it was almost dawn.

In the morning, there was a knock, and when she opened the door, Chase stepped inside. She could smell his aftershave, and it was difficult to resist putting her arms around him and kissing him.

"I wanted to see you before I leave," he said, gazing at her solemnly. "I'm flying out right away. I don't expect to be back here for a while." He handed her a key. "Here's the key to one of the suites, the one I never used. You and your family can use it whenever you want."

"Thank you," she said, taking the key. "I'll miss you," she added softly, trying to maintain control of her emotions and hating to see him leave.

"I still would like you to go with me to Houston. I can fly you back and forth to see your family."

She shook her head, fighting the knot in her throat and the tears that threatened. "Thanks, but no. That's not the life for me, and I have responsibilities here."

While tension mounted between them, he faced her and then closed the distance between them by wrapping her in his arms and kissing her.

Winding her arms around his neck, she poured all her longing and love into her kiss, wanting to make him regret leaving and not forget her. His cell phone rang, and when he ignored it, she pushed against him, stepping out of his embrace.

"Someone wants you," she said. "You go."

As he stepped back, a muscle worked in his jaw. "Bye, Laurel. You know how to reach me."

She nodded, feeling the threat of tears and trying to keep from crying. He turned and left, closing the door behind him, and she covered her face with her hands and cried. "I love you," she whispered.

She didn't want to see anyone until she was more composed, so she left a message on Brice's phone that she was working in her suite and would be in the office later in the morning.

When she did go to the office, she shut herself in to try to pour herself into work and keep her mind off Chase.

Brice was quiet and to her relief never mentioned Chase. When five o'clock came and she could escape to her suite, she spent an hour alone in the quiet of her empty quarters. She missed Chase terribly and kept wondering what he was doing, curious if he was thinking about her. She suspected he was right now, but she didn't think it would last many days. He was a busy person, and she knew before long another woman would take her place, but at the moment she couldn't bear to think about that.

The night was long and lonely, with little sleep, and she was relieved to dress for work the next day. When the phone rang, her heart missed a beat, and she raced to answer it, holding her breath and hoping it would be Chase.

"Is this Laurel Tolson?" an unfamiliar voice asked. Disappointment swamped her.

"Yes, it is," she answered.

"Just a minute, Dr. Kirkwood would like to speak to you."

Her heart missed another beat as she gripped the phone, terrified that something had happened to her dad.

"Laurel? Brett Kirkwood. Your father has regained consciousness, and I thought you'd want to come. He's not clear, but he's awake."

"I'll be right there. Oh, thank heavens!" she exclaimed, joy replacing all the misery she'd been feeling. "Have you called my grandmother?"

"No, I'm leaving that to you."

"Thanks," she cried, shoving her feet into shoes. "I'm on my way. Thank you so much!" She replaced the receiver and called her grandmother as she grabbed her purse and rushed out of the suite.

In less than ten minutes she walked into her

father's room. He was propped up on pillows and still had tubes in him, but his eyes were open and he focused on her. "Dad!" she exclaimed, rushing to him and wanting to throw her arms around him but restraining herself. She squeezed his shoulder lightly.

"Laurel. Love you," he said, sounding exhausted with little lapses between his slurred words, but he recognized her and she was overjoyed.

She held his hand. "I called Gramma and the girls, and they're on their way here. We're all so happy you're better. Just try to get well."

"You here from—?" he frowned as if he couldn't think where she'd been living.

"I've been staying here until you get well."

He squeezed her hand.

"I love you and I know you're going to get well," she said. He looked like a shadow of his former robust self, but now she was certain he would mend.

He closed his eyes and she didn't disturb him. When the doctor came into the room, she walked over to him.

"Thank you for calling me. I talked to him a little and I suppose he's asleep."

"He's come around beyond what we expected.

He's a strong person. I think that in a couple of days you'll see a big difference in him. His vitals are good. His recovery will take time."

"We can hire nurses to care for him at our ranch. I've sold the hotel and financing care for him won't be a problem."

"Good. We'll just have to take it a day at a time and get him back on his feet so he can go to therapy, but one crisis is over."

"Thank heavens!" she exclaimed. "Thanks for all you've done," she added and he nodded, going to the bed to take her father's pulse.

Her father woke and the doctor talked to him briefly and then left. Laurel went back to sit at her father's side. Ten minutes later her grandmother and sisters arrived, and she was happy to see that her father was awake again and could talk a little to each of them.

The family spent the day in his room and then left for dinner together. The moment they sat at their table in a local café, Diana turned to Laurel. "Where's Chase? Want to call him to eat with us?"

"No. He's gone to Texas right now," she said and that ended the conversation, but she saw her grandmother give her a sharp look.

"He's a keeper," Diana said. "I hope you marry him."

She laughed, wishing they could change the subject but trying to avoid announcing that he was out of her life. In minutes she got the conversation on the girls' and their activities, and Chase didn't come up again.

When they parted, she hugged each one. "I'll call you whenever I talk to the doctor again," she said.

"We'll come back tomorrow," her grandmother replied. "This has been a wonderful day. I feel he's turned a corner and will get well."

"I'm sure he will," Laurel said, feeling positive about him. When she returned to her empty suite, she looked at the phone to see if the red light indicated messages, but there were none.

Trying to get her thoughts off Chase, she began to plan her father's move to Billings for physical therapy. Now with Chase's money plus the sale of the hotel, she had far more choices and more resources and they could do what they wanted without financial restraints.

Even with her joy over her father, she couldn't get Chase out of her thoughts, and at night she missed him terribly. She gazed off in the distance, wondering what he was doing at that moment and if he'd missed her much at all. "Chase—" she whispered, longing to see him.

In Houston, Chase swam laps in his pool, pouring all his energy into the swim, trying to work off the hurt he couldn't escape. He missed Laurel and couldn't forget her; it wasn't like any other time in his life when he'd walked out on a relationship. She'd never even been in his Houston home, yet he kept seeing her everywhere, especially when he glanced at his big, empty bed. During the day when he was in public, it had been worse. Every tall, good-looking blonde made him take a second look and wish it were Laurel.

With muscles aching, he stopped and climbed out of the pool. He'd worked out for two hours after getting back from the office. He'd run ten miles this morning. He'd swum laps tonight. And still he couldn't get her out of his thoughts. He was sleeping only a couple of hours at night. "I miss you, dammit," he said to no one.

His phone rang and his hopes jumped that it would be her and she'd changed her mind about moving to Houston.

He yanked up the cell phone and punched a button to take the call, his hopes plummeting when he heard Luke's voice.

"We got a contract on the office building, so now we own the next block and this one," Luke said.

"Good," Chase replied without really thinking about what Luke had told him. "How's Laurel?"

There was only a moment of silence. "She's fine. I heard that her father came out of his coma and she's spending most of her time at the hospital and getting ready to move him to her ranch or Billings. She'll have her hands full, so I don't expect to see her around the hotel. Matter of fact, I heard she's planning on moving out to be with him."

"I'm glad he's recuperating. I didn't think he would."

"You wouldn't think so, but I guess miracles happen. The entire hotel staff is staying, so there won't be any upheaval or transition. I'm going to the field tomorrow, and I'll give you a report about that. If it meets your approval, I'd just as soon put Brice in charge of the hotel and let him report directly to me. He knows the Tolson as well as a person can know a business."

"Do what you think is best," Chase said, still thinking about Laurel.

They talked briefly about business, and then Chase hung up, staring into space, seeing Laurel and wanting her badly. He clenched his fist. What was the matter with him? He'd never been like this over the breakup of a relationship. He hadn't intended for this one to break up, and he wished again that she'd come to Houston with him.

Two more miserable nights and days of grueling workouts and he sat glumly on the side of his empty bed, reaching for the phone as he had over a dozen times each night. He wanted to call Laurel, but he knew there was no point in it because there was no future for them. No future—that was the bleakest thought of all. He rubbed the back of his neck and wondered if he had fallen in love. Really in love. Laurel had been right. In the past it had always been "in lust," but this was different and he was beginning to see that. He wasn't getting over her. If anything, each day grew worse, and if he thought about her going out with another guy, he hurt as if stabbed by a knife. Was he in love?

He shuddered and thought about his dad and his feelings about marriage and his claustrophobia over being tied down. Yet how bad would that be with Laurel? All the time he'd spent with her had been paradise, and he'd never felt claustrophobic or tied down. He'd felt more alive than at any time in his life, and he'd had the best sex life ever, plus he liked being with her and talking things over with her. She had solved the problem of Ty Carson to everyone's satisfaction.

Chase stood impatiently and paced the floor, going to his exercise room to change to shorts and running shoes. As he ran, he continued to mull over his feelings for Laurel.

Could he think about marriage? It gave him a chill, but he thought about when he had been living with Laurel. There had been nothing terrible or confining about their relationship. Far from it. He couldn't wait to get back to her each day.

Was he really in love, and could he possibly face marriage and deal with it? All he knew for certain was that he hurt like hell without her and thought about her constantly. His work was suffering and something had to give.

Each day Laurel's father improved, and she had been amazed at his progress. The third week of September, as she pored over books in her office after sundown, her phone rang and she answered to hear Diana's frantic voice.

"Laurel, it's Gramma. She's fallen and hurt herself, and we've called an ambulance from Athens. I thought you'd want to meet us at the hospital."

"How badly is she hurt?" Laurel asked, cold with fear.

"I don't know. She seems in a lot of pain. She doesn't want to move, and we don't want to move her. She had her hands filled with magazines and stuff she was bringing downstairs, and near the bottom she missed a step and fell. She said it's her foot that hurts."

"Thank goodness it's not her back or her hip! I'll meet you. I'll be waiting at the emergency room entrance," Laurel said. Next, she called Brice to tell him where she'd be, glad he was working a night shift at the hotel.

When she went downstairs, he was waiting. "I'll drive you to the hospital," he said, but she shook her head.

"I'll be fine. Ashley said Gramma is complaining about her foot, so maybe it won't be too bad."

"If you're sure," he said and she nodded.

It was well after two in the morning when she returned to the hotel. Her grandmother had a

broken foot, and they were keeping her over-
night for observation, but otherwise she seemed
fine. Ashley and Diana stayed at the hospital to
spend the night and take their grandmother back
the next day.

Laurel knew they could move into the hotel.
Her grandmother wouldn't have to cook, and they
could have a taxi whenever they needed one. She
lay in bed, mentally making plans that she would
work on the next day. The weekend approached,
and she dreaded it because she would have empty
hours and miss Chase more than ever.

Midmorning Tuesday, the last day of September, she stood in the lobby with Brice and froze
when she turned to look at the front door. Her
heart thudded and she felt for a moment as if she
were dreaming, but it was really Chase Bennett.

Eleven

Breathless, Laurel could only stare. Dimly she heard Brice say goodbye, but she ignored him. Chase was wearing a navy suit, and he looked more handsome than ever—it took all her willpower to keep from running to throw her arms around him.

When she looked at his solemn expression, she suspected he was here to attend to something involving business that wasn't going the way he wanted it. As his gaze swept over her, she became aware that her hair was loosely clipped with strands falling around her face. She wore cream-colored slacks and a white shirt and wished now she'd dressed up more, even though she guessed she would see little of him.

As he walked up to her, she could barely breathe. Her mouth was dry and her heart drummed. She wanted more than anything to reach for him. Instead, she just smiled. "I'm surprised to see you. I didn't think you'd be back."

"Can we go where we can be alone and talk?"

"Sure. Let's go to my office," she said. He walked beside her. "Did you just get in?"

"Yes. I don't think anyone else knows I'm here, although they will by now," he added.

Surprised, she glanced up at him. "You didn't come on business?"

"Yes, of a sort," he answered and reached around her to hold the door open to her office.

Mystified, she stepped inside, catching the scent of his aftershave, which gave her another pang of longing. Memories tugged at her and she locked her fingers together because the temptation to reach for him now that they had privacy was overwhelming.

"You look wonderful," he said, placing his hands on her shoulders.

"Thanks, and I can say the same to you," she answered quietly, putting her hands on his waist instead of hugging him as she wished.

"I've missed you," he admitted, and her heart skipped a beat. His gaze was filled with desire and her lips parted. She leaned closer and then she was in his arms while he kissed her hungrily.

Knowing she was headed for more hurt, she held him tightly while she kissed him. She wanted to make love to him, wanted him to love her, yet she knew that wasn't going to help the situation. Finally she pushed away and gasped for breath. "Why are you here?"

"I had all sorts of plans, but I can't remember them. Dammit, I don't want to be without you. Will you marry me?"

Stunned, she stared at him—her heart took another swoop, missing beats and then racing. The swift rush of joy was instantly snuffed out because it was déjà vu and Chase's reaction would be the same that Edward's had been.

"Chase, I remember long talks about you wanting to avoid responsibility and getting tied down." She knew this would end his proposal as swiftly as he had presented it. "I'm completely tied down and have responsibility for my family. Diana and Ashley are still underage. Gramma fell and broke her ankle and is on crutches, so I'm moving the three of them here to the hotel.

Dad has come out of the coma and soon he'll be moved to Billings for physical therapy; I'm looking at houses there so I can stay with him. I'm shocked you proposed," she said, feeling anguish and expecting him to back off as swiftly as Edward had, even though Chase had known some of her feelings before he proposed.

"I love you, Laurel," he said solemnly. "I've got plenty of money to help, and we can work it out," he said. "You talked about moving them to Texas after your dad finishes therapy. We can move them in with us—"

"You said you never wanted to be tied down with responsibility for a family. Good heavens!" she exclaimed, dazed by the turnaround in his attitude.

"That's before I was really in love. I don't think I'll be 'tied down,'" he replied. "I didn't feel that way when we were together. Maybe I'm beginning to see that my dad did what he wanted all those years."

Shocked, she stared at him. "You were so certain—"

"I'm damn certain I don't want to live without you. I love you," he repeated and pulled her into his arms to kiss her, and this time she let go of her worries and fears and kissed him wildly in return, joy filling her as well as desire sweeping through her as swiftly as a raging fire.

Over an hour later, as she lay in his arms on the sofa in her office, she wiggled. "This is not nearly as large a sofa as the one you had in your office."

"It's large enough for me," he said. "I don't want to let go of you."

"Are you staying the weekend?"

"I can stay or I'll take you to Texas with me so you can see my Houston house."

"I don't think I can leave right now," she answered cautiously, expecting an argument.

"Well, then I'll stay. To hell with business. Let's go up to my suite," he said, sitting up with her on his lap.

"I didn't think you'd ever be in it again."

"I didn't either," he said, looking at her. "Can we shut ourselves away for the rest of the day?"

"I need to cancel some things, and you should really talk to Luke because he'll know you're here. After that we can."

"If you insist," he said with a long sigh. "All right." He stood and pulled on his briefs and trousers while she pulled on lacy underwear and reached for her slacks.

She realized he was standing, watching her dress, and she waved a hand at him. "For heaven's sake! Look the other way."

"Not for a cool million dollars will I look the other way," he said. She wrinkled her nose and pulled on her slacks. "Laurel, you never did give me an answer. Will you marry me?"

"You don't care that I'm a family person?" she asked again.

"Haven't I made that clear?" he replied with a solemn expression.

"Yes, I'll marry you. I love you," she said, giving him a hug, and he kissed her.

"I love you and I hope to spend the rest of our lives showing you. Now dress so we can go upstairs and I can undress you again."

"As quickly as possible," she said, scooping up her blouse. He reached into his pocket.

"I brought you something from Texas," he said, holding out a small bit of pink tissue paper tied with a pink ribbon.

"Thank you," she said, smiling and taking it from him. Curious, she couldn't feel anything in the tiny package. She tore the paper open and looked at a dazzling diamond set in a gold mounting.

"Chase! This is magnificent! Absolutely awesome!" She threw her arms around his neck and kissed him. He kissed her passionately until he stopped abruptly.

"Dammit, let's go upstairs. This is torment and I don't want another round on that sofa or the floor."

She laughed and held out her hand. "You put it on me, please."

He took the ring and held her hand, looking into her eyes. "Laurel, will you be my wife?"

"Yes. I love you and I'll marry you," she said, joy making her laugh. He slipped the huge diamond on her finger. It was dazzling, catching the light and sparkling. "I can't wait to tell my family."

"You can wait a little while," Chase said. "C'mon. Let's get up so I can undress and kiss you."

She laughed and linked her arm in his as she looked at her ring. "Now Brice will apologize for slugging you."

"That wasn't why I proposed," he said and she laughed, squeezing his waist and then taking his arm again. "Laurel, let's marry soon. I don't want to wait a long time."

"Fine with me, but I want my family present and I'd like to meet your family."

"We can call them and we'll go see them as soon as you can get away." In the elevator he pulled her to him. "I love you, darlin'. I can't believe how much I love you. And now you're making me the happiest man on earth."

Epilogue

In October, Laurel stood at the entrance to the sanctuary. Dressed in a long pink organza, her grandmother was seated in front with her crutches at her side and one foot propped up. Diana and Ashley, as well as Becca Carson and Chase's two sisters, Madison and Emma, had already walked down the aisle and were standing at the front.

It was Chase whom Laurel looked at, her heart racing with joy and eagerness. Within minutes she would become his wife. She was still surprised that he was so eager for marriage.

His three brothers, Graham, Justin and Gavin, were groomsmen, along with his cousins Jared and Matt. She smoothed her veil, and the wedding planner straightened the cathedral train of her gown as trumpets blared and the music changed to the wedding march. She took her dad's hand. He was beside her in a motorized wheelchair, and together they went down the aisle.

He gave her to Chase, and she stepped forward to repeat her vows to the tall, handsome man she loved with all her heart.

As if in a daze, after the ceremony she drifted through the photo-taking process. Then they went to the Athens' Country Club for a reception. She removed the train from her dress and finally stepped into Chase's arms for the first dance.

"You're stunning, Laurel," he said, smiling at her as they circled the dance floor.

"And you're breathtakingly handsome, and I can't wait until we're alone."

He groaned. "Let's not talk about that, because I know it's hours and hours away before I'll have you to myself."

"This is the happiest day of my life," she said.

"I think that's my line."

"I'm still reeling with shock that you're settling down to marriage, but you're into it now, mister!" she teased.

"Hot nights with you is not 'settling down.' I can't wait. This is exactly what I want. I was miserable without you, Laurel," he said solemnly, and her heart lurched.

"When do I get to discover where you're taking me for our honeymoon?"

"I hope you like the coast of France."

"With you, I'll love the coast of France," she said as he spun her around.

"Great! After this dance I don't expect to get to talk to you again until we cut the cake, because my dad and then my brothers and cousins will each want to dance with you."

"Your family is wonderful. You cousins are delightful, and I like Jared's wife, Megan. Their son, Ethan, is a great kid."

He smiled at her. "I wish we were alone."

"Both of us do. Time will pass." The music ended and she saw Will Bennett approaching. His brown hair was streaked with gray, and he had a ruddy complexion from many hours spent outside, but he was a handsome man and attention-getting in his pearl-gray cutaway coat and dark trousers. "Here comes your dad."

"And I will go tell your grandmother we'll take her dancing when she's on two feet again."

"May I have this dance?" Chase's father asked and stepped up to take Laurel's hand as a waltz began.

"Welcome to the family," he said, smiling at her. "I'm happy to have you in the Bennett clan, Laurel," he said, gazing at her with eyes as green as his son's. "I had given up on Chase ever marrying, so this is wonderful. I can stop worrying about him now."

She laughed. "It's difficult to imagine anyone worrying over Chase, because he's so supremely confident about what he's doing."

"Even so, his mother and I are deeply thankful you have come into all our lives. You'll be a good influence on him, and he's already settling down."

Laurel chatted with her father-in-law as they danced, glancing often at Chase. She saw Ashley dancing with Chase and she was sure Diana couldn't wait for her turn—despite the fact that both girls had danced with him last night at their rehearsal party.

As the dance ended, Chase joined her briefly. He had shed his gray cutaway coat, and she was eager to change to her regular dress and leave with him. "I'll ask Mom to dance, and here comes Gavin to dance with you."

She glanced around to see Gavin, Chase's twenty-nine-year-old brother, approaching them.

"Now here is a true confirmed bachelor," Chase said, clasping his green-eyed brother on the shoulder. "My best accountant and one who will never succumb to marriage."

"True, bro. May I have the next dance?" he asked Laurel, and she smiled at him as she took his hand.

Just as Chase had said, she danced with his brothers and then with his oldest cousins, Jared and Matt.

It was early afternoon before Chase appeared at her side and took her arm, and they spent another hour telling their families goodbye. Then Laurel changed to a pale yellow silk dress. Finally, they rushed to a waiting white limo and sped away, with the bride instantly in her groom's arms.

"So, where are we spending tonight?" she asked him.

"The closest place we can get to is my coastal home, even though it's in the wrong direction for our honeymoon and will mean longer travel tomorrow. We'll spend tonight on the California coast and tomorrow night in New York City. Then we'll be in France for two weeks. How's that sound for the itinerary?"

"Paradise," she answered, smiling at him and pulling him to her.

It seemed another eternity before they arrived at the house in California. Fog had closed in and moisture dripped from trees. Chase came around the car and opened her door, sweeping her into his arms.

"Luggage. Remember, there's luggage," she said, wrapping her arm around his neck.

"You won't need it tonight," he answered, carrying her to the front door. He handed her the key and lowered her to where she could unlock the door. When they entered, he set her on her feet while he turned off the alarm. He had changed to a new black suit and had shed his coat and tie in the limo and had unbuttoned the top buttons of his shirt.

With every step her pulse sped. She couldn't resist touching him. She was eager to kiss him. His green eyes had darkened when he turned to draw her into his arms. As he kissed her, she felt his hands at her zipper and then her dress fell in a swish around her ankles.

Eagerly, she tugged his shirt out of his trousers and unfastened the buttons, pushing his shirt off his shoulders and trailing her hands over his chest as she looked at him. "I love you, Chase," she whispered.

"I'm going to spend my lifetime trying to keep you happy," he said, holding her away slightly and gazing at her. "You're gorgeous, darlin', and I can't live without you."

She caressed his jaw, thinking she was the luckiest woman on earth. She loved Chase with all her heart.

"Chase, I still can't believe you wanted to marry and that I'm your wife now. It doesn't seem real. You had convinced me completely that you wouldn't do this."

"That was before I fell in love with you, Laurel. And I'm so in love. You can't imagine. Without you, I hurt like I'd never hurt before," he confessed, and her heart thudded.

"You couldn't have hurt any more than I did," she whispered, "but that's over now because we have each other, and as long as I live, I hope you never feel tied down or have regrets."

"I couldn't possibly. I want to love you constantly all during our honeymoon and then as much as possible when we return to our regular lives. I want to be with you the rest of my life. I love you, darlin'. Love you always and forever," he said, and her heart pounded with joy as he pulled her close to kiss her again.

* * * * *